Green Water,

Green Sky

Also available in Laurentian Library:

OKANAGAN COLLEGE LIBRARY
BRITISH COLUMBIA

Green Water,

Green Sky

BY MAVIS GALLANT

74685

Macmillan of Canada
A Division of Gage Publishing Limited
Toronto, Canada

Copyright © 1959 by Mavis Gallant
All rights reserved. The use of any part of this
publication reproduced, transmitted in any form
or by any means, electronic, mechanical,
photocopying, recording, or otherwise, or stored
in a retrieval system, without the prior consent of
the publisher is an infringement of the copyright
law.

First paperback edition published by Macmillan
of Canada, A Division of Gage Publishing
Limited, 1983.

Canadian Cataloguing in Publication Data
Gallant, Mavis
　Green water, green sky
(Laurentian library ; 78)
Originally published: Boston : Houghton Mifflin, 1959.
ISBN 0-7715-9774-6
I. Title. II. Series.
PS8513.A44G73 1983　　　　C813′.54　　　　C83-098657-X
PR9199.3.G348G73 1983

Cover design by Brant Cowie/Artplus

Printed in Canada

to Diarmuid Russell

Ay, now am I in Arden; the more
fool I; when I was at home, I
was in a better place: but
travellers must be content.

AS YOU LIKE IT, ACT II

I

I

I

I

I

THEY WENT off for the day and left him, in the slyest, sneakiest way you could imagine. Nothing of the betrayal to come showed on their faces that morning as they sat having breakfast with him, out on the hotel terrace, a few inches away from the Grand Canal. If he had been given something the right length, a broom, say, he could have stirred the hardly moving layer of morning muck, the orange halves, the pulpy melons, the rotting bits of lettuce, black under water, green above. Water lapped against the gondolas moored below the terrace. He remembered the sound, the soft, dull slapping, all his life. He heard them say at the table they would never come here in August again. They urged him to eat, and drew his attention to gondoliers. He refused everything they offered. It was all as usual, except that a few minutes after he was in an open boat, churning across to the Lido with Aunt Bonnie and Florence. Flor and Aunt Bonnie pushed along to the prow and sat down side by side on a bench, and Aunt Bonnie pulled George toward her, so he was half on her lap. You couldn't sit properly: her lap held a beach bag full of towels. The wind picked up Flor's long pony tail of hair and sent it across George's face. His cousin's hair smelled coppery and warm, like its color. He wouldn't have called it unpleasant. All the same, it was an outrage, and he started to whine: "Where are *they*?" but the wind blew so that you couldn't hear a thing.

He had been on the beach most of the morning before he planted himself in front of Aunt Bonnie in her deck chair and said, "Where've they gone? Are they coming here?"

Aunt Bonnie lowered the book she was reading and regarded George with puckered, anxious face — in his memories, an old face, a frightened face. She sat under a series of disks, in dwindling perspective; first an enormous beach umbrella, all in stripes, then her own faded parasol, then a neutral-colored straw hat. She said, "Well, you know, it's like this, Georgie, they've gone off for the day. They wanted to have one little day on their own. You mustn't be selfish. They're only looking at old pictures. You'd rather be on the beach than looking at pictures . . ."

"I'd sooner be looking at pictures," George said.

". . . so we brought you over to the beach,

said Aunt Bonnie, not even listening. "You mustn't be so selfish all the time. Your mother never has a minute. This trip is no fun for her at all."

Oh, they had managed it beautifully. First they were out on the hot terrace, offering him gondoliers, then he was abandoned with Aunt Bonnie and Flor.

Even years later, when they talked about that day, and his parents wondered how they had found it in them to creep off that way, without warning or explanation; even when they were admitting it was quite the worst thing to do to a child; even then, there was an annoying taint of self-congratulation in their manner. He had been a willful, whiny, spoiled little boy, and some people, Aunt Bonnie for one, claimed that his parents were almost afraid of him. His Fairlie cousins had called him the Monster, while his mother's relatives, more serious and concerned, often said he was being badly prepared for the blows and thumps of life, and wouldn't thank his parents later on. As it happened, George had turned out well. At seventeen, he was a triumphant vindication for his parents of years of hell. Oh, Lord, what he had been at five, his mother liked to say, smiling, shaking her head. At seven! He had ruined their holiday in Venice that time, although they always took all the blame: they should never have gone off for the day, creeping away when his back was turned. It might have marked him for life. *There* was a frightening thought. Like any averted danger, they liked to bring it up. "Do you remember, George, that time in Venice with Bonnie and Flor?"

Of course he remembered. He still had six little cockleshells picked up on the Lido. He remembered the brilliant parasols, askew in the hot wind, and Flor, his cousin, thin, sunburned, fourteen, sitting straight in the center of a round shadow; she sat and scooped sand with her fingers and looked out on the calm sea. George might have drowned for all she cared. He stumped about on the sand by himself, tomato-pink, fair-haired, deeply injured, rather fat. The sea was so flat, so still, so thick with warmth you might have walked on it. He gathered shells: black, brown, cream-and-pink, with minutely scalloped rims. Aunt Bonnie carried them back to Venice for him in her pockets, and now six were left. They were in a shoebox along with a hundred or so other things he would never throw away. He had another remnant of Venice, a glass bead. It came from a necklace belonging to Flor. She bought it that day, at an open stall, just in front of the place where the boat came in from the Lido. The clock on the Piazza began clanging noon, and the air filled with pigeons and with iron sound. They were filing off the boat in orderly fashion when suddenly Flor darted away and came back with the necklace in her hands. Aunt Bonnie hadn't finished saying, "Oh, do you like those glass beads, Flor? Because if you do,

I'd rather get you something decent . . ." The string of the necklace broke an instant later, the first time Flor pulled it on over her head. The glass beads rolled and bounded all over the paving; pigeons fluttered after them, thinking they were grains of corn. The necklace breaking, the hotly blowing wind, excited Flor. She unstrung the beads still in her hands and flung them after the others, making a wild upward movement with her palms. "Oh, stop it," her mother cried, for people were looking, and Flor did appear rather mad, with her hair flying and her dress blowing so that anybody could see the starched petticoat underneath, and the sunburned thighs. And poor little George, suddenly anxious about what strangers might think — this new, frantic little George ran here and there, picking up large lozenge-shaped beads from under people's feet. When he straightened up, hands full of treasure, he saw that Florence was angry, and enjoying herself, all at once. Her hands were still out, as if she wanted to give just anyone a push. But perhaps he imagined that, for she walked quietly beside him, back to the hotel, and told him, kindly, that he could keep all the beads.

He still had one of those beads. He used to roll it about his palm before exams. There were other times, the many times he said, "God, help me this once, and I'll never bother you again," and it was the bead he held on to, and perhaps addressed. It was a powerful charm; a piece of a day; a reminder that someone had once wished him dead but that he was still alive.

Oh, there was no doubt that Florence had wished him dead. After lunch that day he and Flor had hung over rickety wooden railings and watched a small cargo loading what seemed in his memory to be telephone poles; although he must have been mistaken. Flor leaned forward, resting on her thin brown arms. Their faces were nearly level. She turned and looked at him, half smiling, eyes half closed, as people turn and look at each other sunbathing, on hot sand, and he was giving the smile timorously back when he met her eyes, green as water, bright with dislike, and she said, "It would be easy to push someone in right here. I could push you in." He remembered the heavy green water closing out the sky and the weight of clouds. The clouds piled on the horizon moved forward and covered the lagoon. Once he had fallen in the pond at his grandmother's house — the Fairlie grandmother he and Florence had in common. He was sailing a boat and took one false step. The water in this pond was kept dirty for the sake of some dirt-loving mosquito-eating Argentine fish his grandmother cherished — grown fish the size of baby minnows. These darting minnow fish came around him as he lay in the pond, unmoving, and he felt the soft tap of their heads against his cheeks. The most oppressive part of the memory was that he had lain there, passive, with the mossy water over his mouth. He must have been on his back; there was a memory of sky. The gardener heard the splash and fished him out and he was perfectly fine; not on his back at all, but on his face, splashing and floundering.

He didn't think about this in Venice. It was much later when he placed the two memories one on the other, glass over glass. In Venice, he didn't reply: there wasn't time. There wasn't even time for rage or fear. Aunt Bonnie was waiting for them after her afternoon sleep. They were to find her in the Piazza, and feed the pigeons, and listen to the band. He stamped along on fat legs behind Flor, through heat like water, head down. They stopped and weighed themselves on a public scale that told them their fortunes as well as what they weighed. Their fortunes came down on colored cardboard rectangles. George's said, "Do not refuse any invitations this evening," and Flor's said that she must take better care of her liver, and that she would soon be seeing someone off by train. "Mama's waiting," Flor said, throwing her fortune away. She grabbed his arm and made him walk faster. When they came up to Aunt Bonnie, sitting with tea and a plate of little cakes, they were both flushed with heat, but neither of them complained. They were acting in unison, without having been told. They were doing everything to please Aunt Bonnie. George had an instinctive awareness that this aunt loved him, not because he was Georgie Fairlie and

ought to be loved, but because he was a relative,
Aunt Bonnie's brother's son. He understood that
Flor must know her cousins; she mustn't become
too strange. He was conscious of a quality of love
that was a family and not a personal thing. Florence was playing up well too. Earlier, at lunch,
out on the terrace of the hotel, when one of them
said something funny the other laughed much
harder than the joke deserved, and Aunt Bonnie
laughed with a sad, grimacing pleasure that was
painful to see. Her husband, Uncle Stanley, had
been so dreadful to her, he had humiliated her
so deeply that she couldn't live in America; she
couldn't show her face. She was condemned to
live abroad and bring Flor up in some harmful
way: harmful for Flor, that is. That was what
Aunt Bonnie told him, in a high wretched voice,
and Flor listened, bent over her plate, flashing a
glance sideways, now to her mother, now to
George, to see how he was taking it. She listened
as if she had never heard any of it before, although it must have been her daily fare. Flor was
patient; she was patient even with George's stammer. He asked long riddles, stammering like
mad if he thought a waiter might be listening,
and his cousin was good about guessing the an-
swers, even when he had left out some clue, or
given the whole thing away by telling it back-
ward. That laughter, that patience, was for Aunt
Bonnie. George had never been separated from
his parents before and had fugitive thoughts that

they might never come back, but he still understood about Aunt Bonnie, without having been told. It was the first time he had been expected to do anything for anyone in his life.

To please Aunt Bonnie they stood on the edge of the Piazza, not too far away, because she would want to see them enjoying themselves. They shook grain out of newspaper cones and flung it around. Aunt Bonnie watched from her café table, and nodded, and smiled.

Without looking at George, Flor said, "You saw Stanley, didn't you?"

"He came on the boat," said George.

"Was she with him?" said Flor. "What's she like?"

He didn't hedge, as an older person might, and say, "What's who like?" or anything of the kind. He thrust one foot toward a fat, feeding pigeon — taking a stand. He said, "She brought us all different things. She brought me candy."

"I see," said Flor. "They came to see you off. That was loyal of your parents. That was nice." He didn't understand sarcasm. He went on scattering corn. "How old is she?" said Flor, after a time.

"Around thirty-three," said George solemnly, to whom "fifty-eight" or "thirty-one" might have meant much the same. He had heard said of his own mother that she was thirty-three.

"She couldn't even be my mother," said Flor contemptuously. "Mama's forty."

"What fun you're having," came Aunt Bonnie's wailing voice.

They bought new cones of grain and flung it out in an awful rite, in silence. The pigeons were too fat and lazy to fly. They waddled around George's feet, pecking and squabbling and pushing one another away.

"She took it all right," Flor suddenly began again, "until some damn fool went and told her the other one was younger and better looking. She was all right, at first. She even said to me, 'Your father is going to live with this other person. I'm sure she's perfectly sweet.' She couldn't complain," said Flor. "She'd had this man around for ages, this doctor. So she couldn't complain. She used to take me to this doctor for sun lamps on my spine. She must have thought I was deaf and dumb and blind. The nurse of this doctor taught me to play gin rummy. Stanley never said anything and then all of a sudden he blew up and threw her out. Threw us *both* out," said Flor. "Threw her out of the house and she took me too." She was rather affected, telling this, although that was certainly not the word George would have used then. He mistrusted the toss of her head, and the glance she gave, seeing if he was impressed. The effect of this story was to increase his stolidness. He dropped corn one grain at a time, choosing his pigeons. "Nobody was loyal," said Flor. "You stinking Fairlies weren't loyal. You see him all the time. It doesn't matter. She's different now. She never looks at anyone." In George's memory it was here that Florence cried: "She'll never do anything any more. I'll always keep her with me." That wasn't affected. There was no toss of hair, but the same queer pushing attitude of hands he had seen after the necklace broke. She meant these words, they weren't intended for George. It was a solemn promise, a cry of despair, love and resentment so woven together that even Flor couldn't tell them apart.

The paper cones were empty again. This time they threw them away and went back to Aunt Bonnie's table. It was time to listen to the band. Flor ran to her mother and there, in front of everybody, all the strangers and waiters, flung her brown arms around Aunt Bonnie's neck. She cried, "Oh, you look so tired, you look so fed up! Do you hate this place?"

"Darling," said Aunt Bonnie, who had been crying, "it's only for you. You looked so sweet and pretty there with Georgie. I'm sure you hate me. You'll hate me one day. I'm sure I should bring you up some other way. I'm no good at this."

"I'll never hate you, I'll love you," Florence said angrily. "I hate Stanley, I hate George, I hate everybody, I love you."

They sat close so their cheeks were pressed and both of them talked at once and began laughing and crying, with an easiness of emotion, as if they did this a lot. They didn't care about the waiters and they had forgotten George, who stood apart, with an eddy of pigeons around his feet. He loathed his cousin and aunt. He was so embarrassed at what they were doing, he wanted to fly at them and punch them and make them stop. He was alone and ridiculous with pigeons. His parents had gone off for the day without him. They had sneaked off without saying goodbye. It came over him, the hollowness of having been left, the fury at having been made a fool. He dropped his hands to his sides and opened his mouth and howled and howled. His eyes were shut to crescents and his mouth a great cave. He was much too big to be crying this way.

"I've scared him," Florence said, from her mother's side. "I told him something silly, for a joke."

But he wasn't going to let her have the satisfaction of that, and he shut his mouth and opened it again to gasp: "It-wasn't-you," from the circle of waiters and his fluttering aunt, who had sped to take him in her arms. Flor thought he was being honorable, an honorable boy, and she looked at him in a perfect fury of contempt and then turned her back; until both of them were grown, she never really looked at him again. The look was enough to make him stop crying. He waited until his parents returned that evening, apprehensive in their guilt, then he staged the scene all over again, this time sure of the response. He wailed, "You left me all alone," to which Aunt

Bonnie gave an accompanying wail, "My word of honor, he was good as gold," while his mother, rocking him, crooned, "I know, I know," to both.

Flor was dressed for dinner by then, in a dark blue dress. Her arms were bare, her pony-tail hair brushed, coppery, over one shoulder. George's mother stopped mooning over him long enough to stare, admiring — this particular public scene took place in the hotel bar; George was by now getting the hang of attracting and ignoring the public, although he didn't do it so well as Flor — and she exclaimed: "Flor, honey, do something tremendous. You're too pretty to waste."

"Whatever happens," Florence said, composedly, "I shall never marry a Fairlie. I've had enough family. Nothing would persuade me to marry a Fairlie and nothing would persuade me to marry George."

Why this should have made everyone laugh was beyond George: but it became a family expression, brought up, through the years, whenever George and Florence were made to meet. They met summers, two and three years apart, so that every time it was like meeting a different person. Florence paid no attention to him, and they never spoke: although his parents never seemed to notice this. "Flor is sweet," his mother said once, "but she's not like a young girl at all. She's too grown up. I wish Bonnie would send her to college here."

"She wouldn't fit in any more," his father said.

"Anyway, why come back here? She doesn't want to marry a Fairlie."

This reminded George's mother of Venice and she smiled. George was in love with the daughter of the man who owned the garage in the place where they went summers. His parents hadn't started worrying about Barbara Sim: not yet. They still thought it was young and touching and funny; young and funny like George's reply to Florence in the Venice hotel bar: "I'd sooner get nothing for Christmas for nineteen years than marry you."

They met summers: an unreal meeting in hot New York, one year when Bonnie decided to brave it out and then found it was August, nobody there. Once there was a meeting in England, in a hotel, and then somewhere else, on a blowy sandy beach. It was always hot and Aunt Bonnie had a new thing now, migraine headache. Then there was the last meeting, when Flor married a man called Bob Harris she had known in Cannes, and they came back to New York, not creeping this time, but with clatter and circumstance.

They met in an apartment someone had lent the Harris couple. It was full of dark wood and paintings of ships. "This stuff isn't just old," Bob Harris said. "It's period." George didn't hear this: it was repeated to him later on. Because Aunt Bonnie couldn't stand the air-conditioning, the windows were open, the room dense with heat and noise. Most of the people here were Fairlies. George counted eleven persons, including himself, who bore the Fairlie features *in toto:* white hair, white lashes, ruddy cheeks, and, in the case of the less fortunate, the big front teeth. They had come in from everywhere to see the bride. Once you were in the family, you were in to stay: death, divorce, scandal — nothing operated, nothing cut you away. Bob Harris was in it now too. He would fit in, sift down, find his place. Now that he was in there would be no criticism, not a flicker, not a glance. No one would recall that Bonnie had written from Cannes: "Well I don't know what's going to happen now but Florence has gone and married this Jew." When George's mother had read this bit aloud, she had taken on just a shade of Bonnie's whiny accent, that sacred Fairlie drawl, and it came out: "Flounce has gonen married . . ." Nothing else was hinted: nothing survived except their manner of saying "Bob Harris" all the time, as if it were all one word.

There were no Harrises in the room, although Harrises were known to exist. Harris *père* had given Florence a handsome wedding present, and someone had seen his name, quite dignified, on an advertisement for his wine-importing firm. Bob Harris ran the French end of the business: he lived in Paris. He was the same age as Florence, twenty-four. It was the good life. George heard all this and understood. He was part of

this family, so much so that he understood their
hints and suggestions, their stressed words, even
when nothing important was said. It had all been
settled for him in advance: his attitudes and perceptions had been decided for him before he was
born. Perhaps because the room was so crowded
and hot George began to sweat. He felt sweat
breaking on his back and under his arms and
was sure it showed through his clothes. Only, as
it happened, no one was looking at him. They
were much too interested in Florence, who was
really a beauty now, straight and quiet, with
the pretty coppery hair wound in a knot behind her head. They had all been told by Bonnie, separately, as a secret, that there was something wrong with Florence; she could never have
children; she wasn't well. There was a high tide
of noise and Aunt Bonnie's voice above them all.
George and his parents had driven in from the
country and come here late: everyone but Florence was loud and drunk. After a time George
forgot what people might be thinking of him and
he began covertly watching his cousin, from under his whitish lashes, looking for traces of illness, traces of love. He was seventeen that summer and always looking for things. He sat on a
chair at right angles to the sofa on which Florence sat with his aunt. They were holding hands.
He saw that every time Flor's husband came near
her he brushed some part of her skin with the
back of his hand; and that although Flor never

looked at him she was aware of that faintly brushing foreign masculine hand. It was as though some projection of the two, as a couple, was quite apart and in another room, or simply invisible.

"She'll never do anything any more. I'll always keep her with me." This voice came at him, hurled out of the past, with the violence of his cousin's warm hair picked up by the wind and blown across his face.

"Georgie," said Florence, and she bent toward him, the first time she had said anything to him for years, "do you remember how hot it was in Venice when we were kids? I was just reminding Mama. Do you remember that?"

"But New York is *too* hot," said Aunt Bonnie, as if it were somebody's fault.

"Do you remember how green it was all the time?" Flor said to him. "Everything was so clear and green, green water, even the sky looked green to me."

He had been staring, but now he looked inadvertently into her eyes, dark-lashed, green as the lagoon had been — he thought he remembered it now. He couldn't reply. Bob Harris kept moving around, too hospitable, doing too much: at least it seemed so to George, who was sensitive to how people did things. He wanted Bob Harris to be above reproach.

"You were an awful little boy," Flor said to him, smiling. She bent toward him but still held her mother's hand. He had heard about his bratty childhood so often that he no longer minded hearing it. "You wanted so much watching," Flor said. "I think I wasn't a good nursemaid."

He said rather stiffly, "It was only one day."

"But what a day," she said, still smiling, still kind. "You used to run all over the place, like a little mouse. We could hardly keep up."

He said, "I don't remember any of that." His cured stammer returned: "I remember crying in the square."

"I think you cried a lot," said Flor.

"Only once."

The dialogue faltered. They remained in an attitude of conversation, as if posed. "George ought to come over to us in Paris next year," they heard Aunt Bonnie say. "He certainly must do that," Bob Harris chimed in. "He certainly must."

"You know I can't have children?" Florence said, looking George fully in the face. He mumbled a reply. She said, "It was nice of him to want to marry me, all the same."

"Flor," he said, "I've got this bead. It's lucky . . . no, take it . . . I swear, it brings luck . . ." It was out of his pocket and on his wet palm: clear, flawed, the treasure of Venice.

Flor looked at him with a half smile and puckered brows. "What is it, George?" she said clearly, as if to make him stop stammering.

He would have given anything not to have

started this. "You know, you bought this string
of beads? And it broke? When we came back
from the beach? You bought this string of beads
and broke it . . ."

"I'm not a person who breaks things," Flor
said. "I don't remember that."

George said, "We came off the boat, you
know? You went right over to this sort of booth."

"It's just that I'm not a person who breaks
things," Flor said. "Of course, if you say it happened, it's true. I haven't much memory."

"I thought you sort of broke it on purpose," he
said.

"Oh, George," said Flor, shaking her head,
"now I know it can't be real. That just isn't me.
It didn't happen."

He had kept it ten years. He had only to roll
it in his hand or put his eye to the clear flawed
glass and the air was full of pigeons and bells and
the movement of Flor breaking something because she wanted something broken: perhaps
because she was going to be with Aunt Bonnie
for life. Sometimes it was as though Flor had
never left his thoughts, even when he didn't
think of her at all. Because of her, the twin pictures, love and resentment, were always there,
one reflecting the other, water under sky.
Everything had happened as he remembered;
the day had taken place; it had taken its place in
his life. He closed his hand because he thought
he looked rather silly, sitting there, with a loz-

enge of glass on an open palm. Of course it had taken place: look at all these people tangled together, all the Fairlies, and Flor and Bonnie, and now Bob Harris was in it too. And what about his own parents? After that day in Venice they had sworn they would never leave him again, never, ever, and they had kept their word, so that their love for him was a structure, and he was inside. They might have resented it, sometimes. He had: sometimes he had. And now he was going to college and leaving them and maybe the next year he would take that invitation and go to Paris, and the inevitable disloyalty, the faithlessness, the casting-off, made him feel as if he were already at an imagined distance, and remorseful, and starting back.

Flor looked at his closed fist. "Why do people keep things?" she said.

"I don't know," said George. "I guess it proves you were somewhere."

She said, "I feel as if we hadn't ever been in the same place."

"George!" his mother cried from across the room. "Do you remember that time in Venice with Bonnie and Flor?"

"Do you want this?" he said quickly. "It's really yours."

"It wouldn't help me," said Florence. "We weren't ever in the same place. We don't need luck in the same way. We don't remember the same things."

II
II
II
II
II
II

BONNIE MCCARTHY opened a drawer of her dressing table and removed the hat her sister-in-law had sent from New York. It was a summer hat of soft, silken material in a pretty shade of blue: the half-melon hat her sister-in-law had begun to wear at fifteen and had gone on wearing, in various colors and textures, until her hair was gray. This particular melon was designed for travel. It could be folded until it took no more place in a suitcase than a closed fan. Bonnie pushed her lips forward in a pout. She held the hat between thumb and forefinger, considering it. She pulled it on her head, tugging with both hands. The frown, the pout, the obstinate gestures, were those of a child. It was a deliberate performance, and new: after years of struggling to remain adult in a grown-up world, she had found it unrewarding, and, in her private moments, allowed herself the blissful luxury of being someone else.

The hat was a failure. Framed by the chaste blue brim, she seemed slightly demented, a college girl aged overnight. After a long look in the triple mirror, Bonnie said aloud, "This just isn't a normal hat." She dropped it on the table, among the framed pictures and the pots of cream. None of the clothes from America seemed normal to her now, because they no longer came from a known place. She had left her country between the end of the war and the onslaught of the New Look (this is how history was fixed in her memory) and, although she had been back for visits, the American scene of her mind's eye was populated with girls in short skirts and broad-shouldered coats — the war silhouette, 1-85, or whatever it was called. Her recollection of such details was faultless, but she could not have said under which President peace had been signed. The nation at war was not a permanent landscape: Bonnie's New York, the real New York, was a distant, gleaming city in a lost decade. A lost Bonnie existed there, pretty and pert, outrageously admired. This was the Bonnie she sought to duplicate every time she looked in the glass — Bonnie tender-eyed, blurry with the sun of a perished afternoon; Bonnie in her wedding dress, authentically innocent, with a wreath of miniature roses straight across her brow. With time — she was at this moment fifty-two — a second, super-Bonnie had emerged. Super-Bonnie was a classic, middle-aged

charmer. She might have been out of Kipling —
a kind of American Mrs. Hauksbee, witty and
thin, with those great rolling violet blue eyes.
When she was feeling liverish or had had a bad
night, she knew this was off the mark, and that
she had left off being tender Bonnie without
achieving the safety of Mrs. Hauksbee. Then she
would think of the woman she could have been,
if her life hadn't been destroyed: and if she went
on thinking about it too much, she gave up and
consoled herself by playing at being a little girl.

When Bonnie was still under forty, her husband had caught her out in a surpassingly silly
affair — she had not in the least loved the lover
— and had divorced her, so that her conception
of herself was fragmented, unreconciled. There
was Bonnie, sweet-faced, with miniature roses;
wicked Mrs. Hauksbee, the stormy petrel of a
regimental outpost; and, something near the
truth, a lost, sallow, frightened Bonnie wandering from city to city in Europe, clutching her
daughter by the hand. The dressing table was
littered with these Bonnies, and with pictures
of Florence, her daughter. There was Flor as a
baby, holding a ball in starfish hands, and Flor
on her pony, and Flor in Venice, squinting and
bored. To one side, isolated, in curious juxta-
position, were two small likenesses. One was a
tinted image of St. Teresa of the Infant Jesus.
(Bonnie had no taste for obscure martyrs. The
Little Flower, good enough for most Catholics,

was good enough for her.) The Saint had little function in Bonnie's life, except to act as a timid anchor to Bonnie's ballooning notion of the infinite. The second picture was of Bob Harris, Bonnie's son-in-law. It had been taken on the beach at Cannes, two summers before. He wore tartan bathing trunks, and had on and about his person the equipment for underwater fishing — flippers, spear, goggles, breathing tube — and seemed to be a monster of a sort.

When she had done with the hat, Bonnie licked her forefingers and ran them along her eyebrows. She pulled her eyebrows apart and counted twenty times, but when she released the skin, the line between her eyes returned. "La première ride," she said sentimentally. She put on a wry, ironic look: Mrs. Hauksbee conceding the passage of time. When she left the dressing table and crossed the room she continued to wear the look, although she was already thinking about something else. She sat down at a writing table very like the dressing table she had just abandoned. Both were what her son-in-law called "important pieces." Both had green marble tops, bandy legs, drawers like bosoms, brass fittings, and were kin to the stranded objects, garnished with dying flowers in a vase, that fill the windows of antique shops on the left bank of the Seine.

Bonnie was easily wounded, but she had sharp, malicious instincts where other people were concerned. She seldom struck openly, fearing the direct return blow. The petty disorder of her dressing table, with its cheap clutter of bottles and pictures, was an oblique stab at Bob Harris, whose apartment this was, and who, as he had once confided to Bonnie, liked things nice.

She pulled toward her a sheet of white paper with her address in Paris printed across the top, and wrote the date, which was the fifteenth of July. She began: "My darling Polly and Stu — First about the hat. You sweethearts! I wore it today for the first time as it really hasn't been summer until now. I was so proud to say this is from my brother and his wife from New York. Well darlings I am sorry about George I must say I never did hear of anybody ever getting the whooping cough at his age but I can quite see you couldn't let him come over to Paris in that condition in June. Two years since we have seen that boy. Flor asks about him every day. You know those two were so crazy about each other when they were kids, it's a shame Flor was seven years older instead of the other way around. At least we would all be still the same family and would know who was marrying who. Well, nuff said."

So far this letter was nearly illegible. She joined the last letter of each word on to the start of the next. All the vowels, as well as the letters n, m, and w, resembled u's. There were strings

of letters that might as well have been nununu.
Now, her writing became elegant and clear, like
the voice of someone trying on a new accent:
"The thing with him coming over in August is
this, that he would have to be alone with Florence. Bob Harris's father is coming over here
this year, and Bob Harris is going with him to
the Beaujolais country and the Champagne country and I don't know what all countries for their
business, and they will be in these countries all
of August. Now I have been invited to stay with
a dear friend in Deauville for the entire month.
Now as you know Flor is doing this business with
a psychiatrist and she REFUSES to leave Paris.
It wouldn't be any fun for Georgie because Flor
never goes out and wouldn't know where to go
even if she did. It seems to me Georgie should
go to England first, because he wants to go there
anyway, and he should come here around the end
of August when I will be back, and Bob will be
back, and we can take Georgie around. Just as
you like, dears, but this does seem best."

Bonnie was in the habit of slipping little pieces
of paper inside her letters to her sister-in-law.
These scraps, about the size of a calling card,
bore a minutely scrawled message which was
what she really wanted to say, and why she was
bothering to write a letter at all. She cut a small
oblong out of a sheet of paper and wrote in tiny
letters: "Polly, Flor is getting so queer, I don't
know her any more. I'm afraid to leave her alone

in August, but she pulls such tantrums if I say I'll
stay that I'm giving in. Don't let Georgie come,
he'd only be upset. She's at this doctor's place
now, and *I don't even like the doctor.*"

It was three o'clock in the afternoon. Florence
was walking with cautious steps along the Boulevard des Capucines when the sidewalk came up
before her. It was like an earthquake, except that
she knew there were no earthquakes here. It was
like being drunk, except that she never drank any
more. It was a soundless upheaval, and it had
happened before. No one noticed the disturb-
ance, or the fact that she had abruptly come to a
halt. It was possible that she had become invisible. It would not have astonished her at all. Indeed, a fear that this might come about had
caused her to buy, that summer, wide-skirted
dresses in brilliant tones that (Bonnie said) made
her look like a fortuneteller in a restaurant. All
very well for Bonnie, who could be sure that she
existed in black; who did not have to steal
glimpses of herself in shop windows, an existence asserted in coral and red.

At this hour, at this time of year, the crowd
around the Café de la Paix was American. It was
a crowd as apart from Flor as if an invasion of
strangers speaking Siamese had entered the city.
But they were not Siamese: they were her own
people, and they spoke the language she knew
best, with the words she had been taught to use

when, long ago, she had seen shapes and felt desires that had to be given names.

". . . upon the beached verge of the salt flood . . ."

She did not say this. Her lips did not move; but she had the ringing impression of a faultless echo, as if the words had come to her in her own voice. They were words out of the old days, when she could still read, and relate every sentence to the sentence it followed. A vision, clear as a mirror, of a narrowing shore, an encroaching sea, was all that was left. It was all that remained of her reading, the great warehouse of stored phrases, the plugged casks filled with liquid words — a narrowing shore, a moving sea: that was all. And yet how she had read! She had read in hotel rooms, sprawled on the bed — drugged, drowned — while on the other side of the dark window rain fell on foreign streets. She had read on buses and on trains and in the waiting rooms of doctors and dressmakers, waiting for Bonnie. She had read with her husband across from her at the table and beside her in bed. (She had been reading a book, in a café, alone, the first time he had ever spoken to her. He had never forgotten it.) She had read through her girlhood and even love hadn't replaced the reading: only at times.

If Bonnie had been able to give some form to her own untidy life; if she had not uprooted Flor and brought her over here to live — one ma

jestically wrong decision among a hundred in-
decisions — Flor would not, at this moment,
have feared the movement of the pavement under her feet and watched herself in shop windows to make sure she was still there. She would
not have imagined life as a brightly lighted stage
with herself looking on. She would have depended less on words; she would have belonged
to life. She told an imagined Bonnie, "It was always your fault. I might have been a person, but
you made me a foreigner. It was always the
same, even back home. I was the only Catholic
girl at Miss Downland's. That was being foreign."

"What about the Catholic girls from Mexico?"
said Bonnie, from among the crowd before the
newspaper kiosk where Flor had paused to con-
sult, blankly, the front page of the *Times*.

Trust Bonnie to put in a red herring like the
Mexican girls at school: it didn't merit a reply.
Still, the discovery that it had always been the
same was worth noting. It was another clearing
in the thicket that was Dr. Linnetti's favorite
image: another path cleared, another fence
down, light let through. She groped in her purse
for the green notebook in which she recorded
these discoveries, and she sat down on a vacant
chair outside the café.

The table at which she had put herself was
drawn up to its neighbor so that a party of four
tourists could have plenty of room for their

OKANAGAN COLLEGE LIBRARY
BRITISH COLUMBIA

drinks, parcels, and pots of tea. One of the four had even pulled over an extra chair for her aching feet. Florence put her notebook on the edge of the table, pushing an ashtray to one side. The *vertige* she had felt on the street was receding. In her private language she called it "the little animal going to sleep." What was the good of an expression like Dr. Linnetti's "vertigo experienced in the presence of sharp lines and related objects"? The effort of lines to change their form (the heaving pavement), the nausea created by the sight of a double row of houses meeting at the horizon point, the triumph of the little fox, had begun being a torment when she was twelve, and had come to live abroad. In those days, Bonnie had put it down to faulty eyesight, via a troubled liver, and had proscribed whipped cream. Now that it was too late, Florence remembered and recognized the initial siege, the weakening of her forces so that the invader could take possession.

Accepting this, she had stopped believing in Dr. Linnetti's trees, clearings, and pools of light. She was beset, held. Nothing could help her but sleep and the dreams experienced in the gray terrain between oblivion and life — the country of gray hills and houses from which she was suddenly lifted and borne away. Coming into this landscape was the most difficult of all, for they were opposed to her reaching it — the doctor, her mother, her husband. Circumstances were needed, and they were coming soon. In two weeks it would be August, and she would be left alone. Between now and August was a delay filled with perils; her mother hesitating and quibbling, her husband trying to speak. (He no longer attempted to make love. He seemed to have a tenacious faith that one day Dr. Linnetti was going to return to him a new Flor, strangely matured, and more exciting than ever.) This period traversed, she saw herself in the heavy silence of August. She saw her image in her own bed in the silence of an August afternoon. By the dimming of light in the chinks of the shutters she would know when it was night: and, already grateful for this boon, she would think, Now it is all right if I sleep.

"Some people just don't care."

"Ask her what she wants to drink."

"Maybe she's after you, Ed Broadfoot, ha ha."

These were three of the four people on whom Flor had intruded. They thought she was French — foreign, at any rate: not American. She looked away from the notebook in which she had not yet started to write and she said, "I understand every word." A waiter stood over her. "*Madame désire?*" he said insultingly. In terror she scrawled: "Mex. girls wouldn't take baths," before she got up and fled — wholly visible — into the dark café. Inside, she was careful to find a place alone. She was the picture of prudence, now, watching the movements of her hands, the di-

rection of her feet. She sat on the plush
banquette with such exaggerated care that she
had a sudden, lucid image of how silly she must
seem, and this made her want to laugh. She
spread the notebook flat and began to write the
letter to Dr. Linnetti, using a cheap ball-point
pen bought expressly for this. The letter was
long, and changed frequently in tone, now curt
and businesslike, when she gave financial reasons
for ending their interviews, now timid and cajol-
ing, so that Dr. Linnetti wouldn't be cross.
Sometimes the letter was almost affectionate, for
there were moments when she forgot Dr. Linnetti was a woman and was ready to pardon her;
but then she remembered that this cheat was
from a known tribe, subjected to the same indig-
nities, the same aches and pains, practicing the
same essential deceits. And here was this im-
postor presuming to help! — Dr. Linnetti,
charming as a hippopotamus, elegant as the wife
of a Soviet civil servant, emotional as a snail, intelligent — ah, there she has us, thought Flor.
We shall never know. There are no clues.

"What help can you give me?" she wrote. "I
have often been disgusted by the smell of your
dresses and your rotten teeth. If in six months
you have not been able to take your dresses to
be cleaned, or yourself to a dentist, how can you
help me? Can you convince me that I'm not going to be hit by a car when I step off the curb?
Can you convince me that the sidewalk is a safe

place to be? Let me put it another way," wrote
Flor haughtily. Her face wore a distinctly
haughty look. "Is your life so perfect? Is your
husband happy? Are your children fond of you
and well behaved? Are you so happy . . ." She
did not know how to finish and started again:
"Are you anything to me? When you go home to
your husband and children do you wonder about
me? Are we friends? Then why bother about
me at all?" She had come to the last page in the
notebook. She tore the pages containing the letter out and posted the letter from the mail desk
in the café. She dropped the instrument of sep-
aration — the lethal pen — on the floor and
kicked it out of sight. It was still too early to go
home. They would guess she had missed her in-
terview. There was nothing to do but walk
around the three sides of the familiar triangle —
Boulevard des Capucines, rue Scribe, rue Auber,
the home of the homeless — until it was time to
summon a taxi and be taken away.

Florence's husband left his office early. The
movement of Paris was running down. The av-
enues were white and dusty, full of blowing flags
and papers and torn posters, and under traffic
signals there were busily aimless people, sore-
footed, dressed for heat, trying to decide whether
or not to cross that particular street; wondering
whether Paris would be better once the street was
crossed. The city's minute hand had begun to
lag: in August it would stop. Bob Harris loved

Paris, but then he loved anywhere. He had never been homesick in his life. He carried his birthright with him. He pushed into the cool of the courtyard of the ancient apartment house in which he lived (the last house in the world where a child played Czerny exercises on a summer's afternoon), waved to the concierge in her aquarium parlor, ascended in the perilous elevator, which had swinging doors, like a saloon, and let himself into the flat. "Let himself into" is too mild. He entered as he had once broken into Flor's and Bonnie's life. He was — and proud of it — a New York boy, all in summer tans today: like a café Liégeois, Bonnie had said at breakfast, but out of his hearing, of course. She was no fool. The sprawled old-fashioned Parisian apartment, the polished bellpull (a ring in a lion's mouth), the heavy doors and creamy, lofty ceilings, appealed to his idea of what Europe ought to be. The child's faltering piano notes, which followed him until he closed the door on them, belonged to the décor. He experienced a transient feeling of past and present fused — a secondhand, threadbare inkling of a world haunted by the belief that the best was outside one's scope or still to come. These perceptions, which came only when he was alone, when creaking or mournful or ghostly sounds emerged from the stairs and the elevator shaft and formed a single substance with the walls, curtains, and gray light from the court, he knew

were only the lingering vapors of adolescent
nostalgia — that fruitless, formless yearning for
God knows what. It was not an ambience of mind
he pursued. His office, which was off the
Champs-Elysées, in a cake-shaped building of
the thirties, was dauntingly new, like the lounge
of a dazzling Italian airport building reduced in
scale. The people he met in the course of business were sharp with figures, though apt to as-
sume a monkish air of dedication because they
were dealing in wine instead of, say, paper bags.
There was nothing monkish about Bob: he knew
about wine (that is, he knew about markets for
wine); and he knew about money too.

Nothing is more reassuring to a European than
the national who fits his national character: the
waspish Frenchman, the jolly Hollander, the
blunted Swiss, the sly Romanian — each of these
paper dolls can find a niche. Bob Harris corre-
sponded, superficially, to the French pattern for
an American male — "un grand gosse" — and so
he got on famously. He was the last person in the
world to pose a problem. He was chatty, and
cheerful, and he didn't much care what people
did or what they were like so long as they were
good-natured too. He frequented the red-inte-
riored bars of the Eighth Arrondissement with
cheerful friends — more or less Americans trying to raise money so as to start a newspaper in
the Canary Islands, and apple-bosomed starlets
with pinky-silver hair. Everyone wanted some-

thing from him, and everyone liked him very much. Florence's family, the indefatigable nicknamers, had called him the Seal, and he did have a seal's sleek head and soft eyes, and a circus seal's air of jauntily seeking applause. The more he was liked, and the more he was exploited, the more he was himself. It was only when he entered his darkened bedroom that he had to improvise an artificial way of thinking and behaving.

His wife's new habit of lying with the curtains drawn on the brightest days was more than a vague worry: it seemed to him wicked. If ever he had given a thought to the nature of sin, it would have taken that form: the shutting-out of light. Flor had stopped being cheerful; that was the very least you could say. Her sleeping was a longer journey each time over a greater distance. He did not know how to bring her back, or even if he wanted to, now. He had loved her: an inherent taste for exaggeration led him to believe he had worshiped her. She might have evaded him along another route, in drinking, or a crank religion, or playing bridge: it would have been the same betrayal. He was the only person she had trusted. The only journey she could make, in whatever direction, was away from him. Feeling came to him in blocks, compact. When he held on to one emotion there was no place for another. He had loved Flor: she had left him behind. It had happened quickly. She hadn't cried warn-

ing. He accepted what they told him — that Flor
was sick and would get over it — but he could
not escape the feeling that her flight was deliberate and that she could stop and turn back if she
tried.

He might have profited by her absence, now,
to go through her drawers, searching for drugs or
diaries or letters — something that would in-
dicate the reasons for change. But he touched
nothing in the silent room that was not his own.
Nothing remained of the person he had once seen
in the far table of the dark café in Cannes, elbows
on table, reading a book. She had looked up and
before becoming aware that a man was watching
her let him see on her drowned face everything
he was prepared to pursue — passion, discipline,
darkness. The secrets had been given up to Dr.
Linnetti — "A sow in a Mother Hubbard," said
Bonnie, who had met the lady. He felt obscurely
cheated; more, the secrets now involved him as
well. He would never pardon the intimacy ex-
posed. Even her physical self had been trans-
formed. He had prized her beauty. It had made
her an object as cherished as anything he might
buy. In museums he had come upon paintings of
women — the luminous women of the Impres-
sionists — in which some detail reminded him of
Flor, the thick hair, the skin, the glance slipping
away, and this had increased his sense of possession and love. She had destroyed this beauty,
joyfully, willfully, as if to force him to value her

on other terms. The wreckage was futile, a vandalism without cause. He could never understand and he was not sure that he ought to try.

His mother-in-law was in the drawing room, poised for discovery. She must have heard him come in, and, while he was having a shower and changing his clothes, composed her personal tableau. The afternoon light diffused through the thin curtains was just so. Bonnie was combed, made up, corseted, prepared for a thousand eyes. Her dress fitted without a wrinkle. She was ready to project her presence and create a mood with one intelligent phrase. She had been practicing having colored voices, thinking blue, violet, green, depending on the occasion. Her hands were apart, hovering over a bowl of asters — a bit of stage business she had just thought up.

If Bonnie had not been the mother of Flor, and guilty of a hundred assaults on his generosity and pride, he might have liked her. She was ludicrous, touching, aware she was putting on an act. But a natural relationship between them was hopeless. Too much had been hinted and said. She had wounded him too deeply. He had probably wounded her. She greeted the young man as if his being in his own apartment were a source of gay surprise, and he responded with his usual unblinking reverence, as if he were Chinese and she a revered but long-perished ancestor; at the same time, he could not stop grinning all over his face.

The effect of discovery was ruined. Bonnie had dressed and smiled and spoken in vain. Even the perfect lighting was a lost effect: the sun might just as well set, now, as far as Bonnie was concerned. She was only trying to look attractive and create a civilized, attractive atmosphere for them all, but nobody helped. He saw that she was once more offended, and was sorry. He offered her a drink, which she refused, explaining in a hurt voice that she was waiting for tea.

"Where's Flor?"

"*You* know," said Bonnie. On the merits of Dr. Linnetti they were in complete accord.

He sat down and opened the newspaper he had brought home. Bonnie gave a final poke at the flowers and sat down too, not so far away that it looked foolish, but leaving a distance so that he need not imagine for one second Bonnie expected him to *talk*. He looked at his paper and Bonnie thought her thoughts and waited for tea. She was nearly contented: it was a climate of mutual acceptance that had about it a sort of coziness: they might have been putting up with each other for years. The room seemed full of inherited furniture no one knew how to get rid of; yet they had taken the apartment as it was. They were trailing baggage out of a fabricated past. The furnishings had probably responded to Bob's need for a kind of buttery comfort; and the colors and textures reflected Bonnie's slightly lady-taste that ran to shot silk, pearly porcelain, and peacock green. Afloat on polished tables were the objects she had picked up on her travels, bibelots in silver and glass. There was a television set prudishly hidden away in a lacquered cabinet, and on the walls the paintings Bob had purchased. It was not a perfect room, but, as Bonnie often told her sister-in-law in her letters, it could have been so much worse. There was nothing in it of Flor.

When Flor came in a few minutes after this there was someone with her: a tall, round-faced young woman with blond hair, whose dress, voice, speech, and manner were so of a piece that she remained long afterward in Bob's memory as "The American," as though being American were exceptional or unique. Flor hung back. The visitor advanced into the room and smiled at them: "I'm Doris Fischer. I live down below. It's marvelous to find other Americans here."

"We met on the stairs," said Flor seriously.

"Met on the stairs, Flor? Met on the stairs?" Bonnie sounded fussed and overcontained, as if she might scream. Flor never spoke to strangers and, since spring, had given up even her closest friends. The two young women seemed about to reveal something: for an instant Bonnie had the crazy idea that one of the two had been involved in a fatal accident and that the other was about to describe it. That was how you became, living with Flor. Impossible, illogical pictures leaped upward in the mind and remained fixed, shining with more brilliance and clarity than the obvious facts. Later she realized that this expectation of disaster was owing to a quality in the newcomer. Doris Fischer, so assertive, so cheerfully sane, often took on the moody gestures of an Irish actress about to disclose that her father was a drunkard, her brother an anarchist, her mother a saint, et cetera. It gave a false start to her presence: any portentiousness was usually owing to absent-mindedness or social unease, although that could be grave enough.

"We were both down there waiting for the elevator," said Doris, in her friendly, normal way. "It was stuck some place. You know how it never works in this building . . ." They had started to climb the stairs together, and she had spoken to Flor. That was all. It was quite ordinary, really.

In Flor's mind, this meeting was extraordinary in the full sense of the word. That any one should accost and speak to her assumed the proportions of fatality. She had been pinpointed, sought out, approached. In her amazement she grasped something that was not far wrong: she had been observed. Doris Fischer had been watching the comings and goings of these people for days, and had obtained from the concierge that they were American. Thoughts of simply presenting herself at their door had occurred and been rejected: wisely, too, for Bonnie would not have tolerated that. This spider role was contrary to Doris's nature. She was observing when she wanted to be involved, and keeping still when everything compelled her to cry, "Accept me!" She was a compatriot and lonely and the others might take her at that value, but Flor's perspective was not wholly askew. Doris was like a card suddenly turned out of the pack: "Beware of a fair-haired woman. She attaches herself like a limpet to the married rock." She would want them all, and all their secrets. She would fill the idleness of her days with their affairs. She would disgorge secrets of her own, and the net would be woven and tight and over their heads.

Everyone remained standing. The fairly mundane social occasion — the person who lived downstairs coming to call — was an event. Doris Fischer saw the husband and the mother as standing forms against the hot summer light. Her eyes were dazzled by the color in the room. The chandelier threw spectrums over peacock walls; blue silk curtains belled and collapsed. Doris thought the room itself perfectly terrible. Her own taste rotated on the blond-wood exports from sanitary Sweden; on wrought-iron in its several forms; on the creeping green plants that prosper in centrally heated rooms but die in the sun. Nothing in her background or her experience could make her respond to the cherished object or the depth of dark, polished wood. She saw there were modern paintings on the walls, and was relieved, for she disliked the past. Radiating confidence now, she stepped farther inside, pointed at the wall opposite, and accused something hanging there.

"It's very interesting," she said, in an agreeable but slightly aggressive voice. "What is it? I mean, who's it by?"

"It is by an Australian who is not yet recognized in his own country," said Bob. He often spoke in this formal manner, never slurring words, particularly when he was meeting someone new. He considered Doris's plain brown-and-white shoes, her plain shirtwaist dress of striped blue cotton, her short, fluffy hair. He was anything but aggressive. He smiled.

They all turned to the painting. Bonnie looked at a bright patch on the bright wall, and Doris at something a child of six might have done as well. Flor saw in the forms exploding with nothing to hold them together absolute proof that the universe was disintegrating and that it was vain and foolish to cry for help. Bob looked at a rising investment that, at the same time, gave him aesthetic pleasure; that was the way to wrap up life, to get the best of everything. Quite simply, he told the price he had paid for the painting last year, and the price it would fetch now that the artist was becoming known: not boasting, but showing that a taste for beauty paid — something like that.

Distress on the fringe of horror covered the faces of the three women, like a glaze, endowing

them with a sudden, superficial resemblance.
Florence's horror was habitual: it was almost
her waking look. Bonnie suffered acutely at her
son-in-law's trampling of taste. Doris, the most
earnest, thought of how many children in vague,
teeming, starving places could have been nour-
ished with that sum of money. Doris stayed to
tea; they kept her for dinner. She came from
Pennsylvania but had lived in New York. She
knew no one Bonnie knew, and Bob thought it
typically wicked of his mother-in-law to have
asked. They were all in a strange land and out
of context. Divisions could be recognized; they
needn't be stressed. Doris said that her husband
was a cameraman. Sometimes she said "cameraman," sometimes "film technician," sometimes "special consultant." He was in Rome on a
job, and would be there all summer. Doris had
decided to stay in Paris and get to know the
place; when Frank was working, she only got in
his way. She was imprecise about the Roman
job. A transferred thought hovered like an insect
in the room: She's lying. Bonnie thought, He's
gone off with a girl: Bob thought, They're broke.
He's down there looking for work. Doris was
clumsy and evasive, she was without charm or
fantasy or style, but they insisted she stay. Flor
could do with an American friend.

In honor of the meal, Doris went home and
returned wearing some sort of finery. She looked
like a social worker going to the movies with a
girl friend, Bonnie thought. Unjust appraisal al-

ways made her kind: she all but took Doris
in her arms. Doris was surprised at the meal,
which was scanty and dull. She was accustomed
to the food of her childhood, the hillocks of
mashed potatoes, the gravy made with cream;
she knew the diet of a later bohemia, spaghetti
with wine and the bottles saved for candlehold-
ers. She could not decide if these well-to-do people were ascetic or plain stingy. Flor ate next to
nothing. Doris looked at her over the table and
saw a bodiless face between lighted candles —
a thin face and thick, lusterless hair. They had
lighted the candles without drawing the curtains,
and, as the summer night had not yet descended,
the room was neither dark nor light, which, for
some reason, Doris found faintly disturbing. The
dining room was Chinese: throughout the
meal she was glared at by monsters. It was
enough to put anybody off. Bonnie chattered
and nervously rattled the little bell before her.
Bob was all indifference and charm. He couldn't
stop charming people: it was a reflex. But
it didn't mean much, and Doris left him cold.
She sensed this, and wished she could make him
pay. She would have been distant and mysterious, but she had already talked too much
about herself. She had given it all away first go.
They had bantering jokes together, underneath
which moved a river of recognition. Bonnie listened to them with a glued smile, and fell into a
melancholy state of mind, wondering if she were
to spend the rest of her life with moral, mental,

social, and emotional inferiors. She thought
these two were perfectly matched. Actually, they
were alike, but not in a way that could draw them
together. Neither Bob nor Doris had much feeling for the importance of time: either of them
could have been persuaded that the world began
the day he was born. It was not enough on which
to base a friendship; in any case, Doris had decided she was chiefly interested in Flor. One day
she would ask Flor if Bob really loved her, and if
he had any intellectual interests other than painting, and what they talked about when they were
alone, and if he was any good in bed. This was
the relationship she was accustomed to and sorely
missed: warm, womanly, with a rich exchange of
marital secrets. She smiled at Flor, and Bonnie
intercepted the smile and turned it toward herself.

"Florence is spending August in Paris," Bonnie
said, with a curved, smiling, coral-colored voice.
"True Parisians prefer the city then." Bob Harris
looked at his mother-in-law and was visibly
shaken by a private desire to laugh. His mother-
in-law stopped being Mrs. Hauksbee and
glared. It seemed to Doris good-humored
enough, though exclusive. She wondered if Flor
was pregnant, and if that was why Flor was so
quiet.

That night, Bonnie got the invitation to Deauville out of the bottom tray of her jewelry case,
where she kept letters, medical prescriptions,

and the keys to lost and forgotten trunks. She scarcely knew the woman who had sent it. They had met at a party. The signature evoked a fugitive image: thin, dark, sardonic, French. She began saying to herself, I hardly know Gabrielle, but it was a case of affinity at first sight.

Gabrielle — the Frenchwoman — had rented a villa at Deauville. She was inviting a few people for the month of August, and she stated in her letter what Bonnie's share of costs would be. Bonnie was not offended. Possibly she had always wanted this. She sat at her dressing table, in her lace-and-satin slip, and read the letter. She wore horn-rimmed reading glasses, which gave her appearance an unexpected dimension. When she looked up the mirror reflected her three ways. Her nose was pointed; underneath her chin hung a slack, soft little pouch. She saw clearly what Gabrielle was and who the other guest would be and that she had been selected to pay. She saw that she was no longer a young woman, and that she depended for nearly everything material on a son-in-law she had opposed and despised. She closed her eyes and put the edge of the letter between her teeth. She emptied her mind, as if emptying a bottle, and waited for inspiration. Inspiration came, as warm as milk, and told her that she had been born a Fairlie, that her husband had ill-used her, that her daughter had made a *mésalliance,* and possessed a heart as impierceable as a nutmeg, whereas Bonnie's heart was a big, floppy cush-

ion in which her loved ones were forever sticking
needles and pins. This daughter now bore the
virus of a kind of moral cholera that threatened
everyone. Inspiration counseled Bonnie to fly,
and told her that her dingy aspirations might
save her. She opened her eyes but did not look
at herself in the glass, for she no longer knew
which Bonnie she expected to see. She said aloud,
in an exceedingly silly voice, "Well, everybody
deserves a little fun."

Later, she said to Flor: "I won't feel so badly
about leaving you, now that you've got this nice
friend." She made this sound as casual as she
could.

Flor gave no sign. She was cunning as a murderer: "If I seem too pleased, she'll be hurt, she
won't go away." She imagined the hall filled with
suitcases and someone coming up the stairs to
carry them away.

Flor had given as her reason for spending
August in Paris that Dr. Linnetti had deemed it
essential. Even if she went away, she would have
to continue paying for the three weekly appoint-
ments. She related the story, now firmly en-
sconced in modern mythology, of Dr. Freud's pa-
tients, and how they all went skiing at the same
time every year, and all broke their legs in the
same way, without warning, and how, as a result
of his winter difficulties, a tradition of payment
while on holiday had become established. If she
left Dr. Linnetti in the lurch, Dr. Linnetti might

resent her, and then where would they all be?
"Morally, it stinks," said Bob. He threatened to
go and see the doctor, but Flor knew he wouldn't.
He had insisted on treating the whole thing as
nothing at all, hoping it would become nothing,
and he would not have committed a positive act.
Bonnie now began talking about Flor's August in
Paris quite gaily, as a settled event, which left
Bob without an ally. He was perplexed. His father was expected from New York any day now.
He could not leave his wife alone in Paris,
he could not really take her with him on a long
business trip, and he did not want his father to
see what Flor, or their marriage, had become.
He had depended on Bonnie, whose influence
had seldom failed. After a time he understood
about Deauville. Bonnie knew that he understood. She remembered the philosophy of self-
sacrifice she had preached, and that still moped
in a corner of their lives like a poor, molting bird.
She would have smothered if she could this old
projection of herself; but it remained, indestruct-
ible as the animal witness in a fairy tale. Bob
ignored her now. He seemed to have turned his
back. He continued to offer holiday pictures to
Flor with accelerated enthusiasm: Spain, Portu-
gal, Portofino, Lausanne, Scotland, gaudy as posters, and as unsubstantial, were revealed and
whisked away. "I have to stay here," she said.
He obtained nothing more.

Because of Bob's nagging, Bonnie became

possessed with the fear that Flor might decide not to stay alone after all, and oblige Bonnie to take her to Deauville. This was hardly feasible, seeing how queer Flor had become. She was likely to say and do anything. She had always been a moody girl, with an unpredictable temper, but that was the personality that went with red hair. Then, too, she had been pretty: a pretty girl can get away with a lot. But, since spring, she had floated out of Bonnie's grasp: she dressed oddly, and looked a wraith. If she did queer things in front of these people at Deauville, Bonnie felt she wouldn't know where to hide from shame. If Flor and Doris Fischer became good friends, Flor might remain more easily in Paris, doing all the sensible things, chatting away to Dr. Linnetti, visiting couturiers with Doris, eating light lunches of omelet and fruit, and so forth. Diet was of great importance in mental equilibrium: you are what you eat. Friendship mattered, said Bonnie, not losing sight of Doris: friendship, rest, good food, relaxing books. In the autumn, Flor would be a different girl.

Flor heard and thought, I used to believe she was God.

Five days remained. Bonnie was rushed off her feet and wore an expression of frank despair. She had left essential duties such as hair, nails, massage, until the end, and every moment was crowded. Nevertheless, because of the importance of the Flor-Doris friendship, she accepted

Doris's suggestion one day that they all three go
for a walk. Doris liked wandering around Paris,
but when she walked alone, she imagined North
Africans were following her. Being fair, she was
a prize. She might be seized, drugged, shipped
to Casablanca, and obliged to work in a brothel.
Even in New York, she had never taken a taxi
without making certain the window could be
lowered. This cherished fear apart, she was sensible enough.

The three women took a taxi to the Place de la
Concorde one afternoon and walked to the Pont
Neuf. They crossed to the Left Bank over the
tip of the Ile de la Cité. It was a hot, transparent
day; slumbering summer Paris; a milky sky, a
perspective of bridges and shaking trees. Flor
had let her long hair free and wore sandals on
her feet. She seemed wild, yet urban, falsely
contrived, like a gypsy in a musical play. Bonnie
walked between the two girls and was shorter
than both. She was conscious only of being
shorter than Flor. It was curious, being suddenly
smaller than the person over whom you had once
exercised complete control. Bonnie's step was
light: she had been careful to keep a young figure. Doris, the big blond, thought she looked
beaky and thin, like a bird. A mean little bird,
she amended. There was something about Bonnie she didn't like. Doris wore the dress they had
come to consider her day-duty uniform: the neat,
standard shirtmaker. Bonnie's little blue hat

would have suited her well. Bonnie thought of
this, and wondered how to offer it. Doris
expressed from time to time her sense of well-
being on this lovely day. She said she could
hardly believe she was really alive and in Paris.
It was like that feeling after a good meal, she said,
sincerely, for the gratification of her digestion
compared favorably with any pleasure she had
known until now. Although neither Flor nor
Bonnie answered, Bonnie had an instant's awareness that their reaction to Doris was the same:
they needn't share a look, or the pressure of
hands. Later, this was one of her most anguished
memories. She forgot the time and the year and
who was with them, remembering only that on a
lost day, with her lost, loved, girl, there had existed a moment of unity while crossing a bridge.

Flor was letting herself see in high, embossed
relief, changing the focus of her eyes, even
though she knew this was dangerous. Human
cunning was keeping the ruin of Paris concealed.
The ivy below Notre Dame had swelled through
the city's painted crust: it was the tender covering
of a ruin. The invasion of strangers resembled
the busloads of tourists arriving at Pompeii.
They were disoriented and out of place. Recording with their cameras, they tried not to live the
day but to fix a day not their own. It had so little
to do with the present that something she had
suspected became clear: there was no present
here, and the strangers were perfectly correct to

record, to stare, to giggle, to display the unease a healthy visitor feels in a hospital — the vague fear that a buried illness might emerge, obliging one to remain. Her heart had left its prison and was beating under her skin. The smell of her own hands was nauseating. Nobody knew.

When they reached the opposite shore, Bonnie decided the walk had gone on long enough. She began looking for a taxi. But Flor suddenly said she wanted to continue. The others fell in step: three women strolling by the Seine on a summer's day.

"There is a window with a horse in it," Florence said seriously. "I want to see that."

Bonnie hoped Doris hadn't heard. There was nothing she could do now. Her daughter's eyes were wide and anguished. Her lips moved. Bonnie continued to walk between the two young women so that any conversation would, as it were, sift through her.

"Didn't we walk along here when I was little?" said Flor.

Flor never spoke of the past. To have her go into it now was unsettling. It was also a matter of time and place. It was four o'clock, and Bonnie had a fitting with her dressmaker at five. She said, "Oh, honey, we never came to Paris until you were a big girl. You know that."

"I thought we used to come along here and look at the horse."

This was so bizarre, and yet Bonnie could not

help giving Doris an anxious, pathetic glance, as if to say, "We used to do things together — we used to be friends." They were still on the Quai de Montebello when Flor made them cross the street and led them to a large corner window. Well, there was a stuffed horse. Flor wasn't so crazy after all.

An American woman, dressed rather like Doris, stood before the window, holding a child by the hand. Crouched on the pavement, camera to his eyes, was the husband, trying to get all of them in the picture — wife, child, horse. The boy wore a printed shirt that matched his father's, and his horn-rimmed glasses were the same, but smaller. He looked like the father reduced. Doris's delighted eyes signaled that this was funny, but Bonnie was too bothered with Flor to mind: Flor looked at the child, then at the horse, with a fixed, terrified stare. Her skin had thickened and paled. There was a film of sweat on her cheeks.

The child said, "Why's the horse there?" and the mother replied in a flat bored voice, "*I* dunno. He's dead."

"That's wrong," said Flor harshly. "He's guarding the store. At night he goes out and gallops along the river and he wears a white and red harness. You can see him in the parks at night after the gates are locked."

Doris, joining in what she imagined the play of a whimsical mind, said, "Ah, but if the gates are locked, how do you get in to see him?"

"There's a question!" cried Bonnie gaily.

She was not listening to her own voice. Everything was concentrated on getting Flor away, or getting the three open-mouthed tourists away from her.

"We did come here when I was little," said Flor, weeping, clasping her hands. "I remember this horse. I'm sure I remember. Even when I was playing in the grass at home I remembered it here." She saw the leafy tunnels of the Tuileries on an autumn day, and the galloping horse: she could not convey this picture, an image of torment, nostalgia, and unbearable pain.

"Oh, love," said her mother, and she was crying now too. There was something in this scene of the old days, when they had been emotional and close. But their closeness had been a trap, and each could now think, If it hadn't been for you, my life would have been different. If only you had gone out of my life at the right time.

Doris thought: Spoiled. Fuss over nothing. She also thought, I'm like a sister, one of the family. They say anything in front of me.

Perhaps this was true, because it seemed natural that Doris find a taxi, take them home, and put Flor to bed. She even ordered a nice cup of coffee all around, putting on a harmless comedy of efficiency before the cook. By now, after a few days, she might have known them for years. She came into their lives dragging her existence like a wet raincoat, and no one made a move to keep her out. She called them by their Christian

names and had heard Bonnie's troubles and
hinted at plenty of her own. Bob referred to
her as Moonface because she was all circles,
round face, round brown eyes. The first impression of American crispness had collapsed. Her
hair often looked as if mice had been at it. The
shirtmaker dresses were held together with pins.
Dipping hems had been stitched with thread the
wrong color. She carried foolish straw baskets
with artificial flowers wound around the handle,
and seemed to have chosen her clothes with three
aims in mind: they mustn't cost much, they must
look as if anybody could wear them, and they
must be suitable for a girl of sixteen. She did not
belong in their lives or in the Paris summer. She
belonged to an unknown cindery city full of used-
car lots. She sat by Flor's bed, hunched forward,
hands around her knees. "I know how you feel
in a way," she said. "Sometimes I feel so depressed I honestly don't like going out on the
street. I feel as if it's written all over me that
something's wrong. I get the idea that the mob
will turn on me and pull me apart because I'm
unhappy and unhappiness is catching." She
seemed genial and lively enough, saying this.
She was fresh from a different world, where gen-
eralized misery was possibly taken for granted.
Bob said that Moonface was stupid, and Flor, for
want of any opinion, had agreed, but could Flor
be superior? She would have given anything to
be a victor, one of that trampling mob

There wasn't much to be had from Flor, and Doris turned to Bonnie instead. She would try every member of the family in turn, and only total failure would drive her away. Within the family, on whatever bankrupt terms, she was at least *somewhere*. She had been afraid of never knowing anyone in Paris: she spoke very little French, and had never wanted to come abroad. But it was not long before she understood that even though they had lived here for years, and used some French words in their private family language, they were not in touch with life in France. They had friends: Bob and Bonnie seemed to go about; but they were not in touch with life in the way Doris — so earnest, so sociologically minded — would have wanted. Still, she enjoyed the new intimacy with Bonnie. For the few days that remained, she had tea every day in Bonnie's bedroom. Bonnie was packing like a fury now. They would shut themselves up in the oyster-colored room, Bonnie dressed in a slip because a dress was a psychological obstacle when she had something to do, and gossip and pack. Doris sat on the floor: the chairs were laden with the dresses Bonnie was or was not going to take to Deauville. Bonnie was careful to avoid dropping the Deauville hostess's name, out of an inverted contempt for Doris, but Doris got the point very soon. She was not impressed. She suspected all forms of titled address, and thought Bonnie would have been a nicer and more sincere person if she had used her opportunities to cultivate college professors and their wives.

Bonnie didn't care what Doris thought. Everything was minimal compared with Flor's increasing queerness and her own headlong and cowardly flight. She talked about Flor, and how Flor was magnifying Bonnie's failings for Dr. Linnetti.

"All children hate their parents," said Doris, shrugging at this commonplace. She was sewing straps for Bonnie. She bit off a thread. There were subjects on which she permitted herself a superior tone. These people had means but were strictly uneducated. Only Bob had a degree. As far as Doris could make out, Flor had hardly even been to school. Doris was proud of her education — a bundle of notions she trundled before her like a pram containing twins. She could not have told you that the shortest distance between two points was a straight line, but she did know that "hostility" was the key word in human relations, and that a man with an abscessed tooth was only punishing himself.

"All I can say is I adored my mother," said Bonnie. "That's all I can say."

"You haven't faced it. Or else you don't remember."

Bonnie remembered other things: she remembered herself, Bonnie, at thirty-seven, her name dragged in the mud, vowing to Flor she would never look at a man again; swearing that Flor could count on her for the rest of her life. She had known in her heart it was a temporary promise and she had said, "I still have five good years." At forty-two, she thought, My life isn't finished. I still have five good years. And so it had been, the postponement of life five years at a time, until now Flor was married and in a dream, and Bonnie was fifty-two. She wanted Flor to hold off; to behave well; not to need help now, this very minute. She was pulled this way and that, now desperate for her own safety, now aghast with remorse and the stormy knowledge of failure. She left Doris sitting on the floor and went into her daughter's room. Flor was lying on the bed, wide-eyed, with a magazine. She kept a magazine at hand so that she could pretend to be reading in case someone came. None of them liked her habit of lying immobile in the semi-dark.

Bonnie sat down on the bed. She wanted to say, Flor, I've had a hell of a life. Your father was a Catholic. He made me be a Catholic and believe a lot of things and then he left off being one and divorced me. And that isn't everything, it's only a fragment. What she said was: "Darling, I'm not going to suggest you see a priest, because I know you wouldn't. But I do agree with Bob, I don't think Dr. Linnetti is any good. If you're going to stay here in August anyway you should see someone else. You know, I used to know a doctor . . ."

"I know," said Flor, loathing awakened.

But Bonnie hadn't meant that old, disastrous love affair. She had meant a perfectly serious professional man out in Neuilly. Flor's eyes alarmed her. She fingered the magazine between them and thought of the other doctor, the lover, and wondered how much Flor had seen in those days. Flor must have been eleven, twelve. She felt as though she had been staring in the sun, the room seemed so dark.

"You see," said Flor, "I'm perfectly all right and I don't need a priest. Mama. Listen. I'm all right. I'm slightly anemic. It makes me pale. Don't you remember, I was always a bit anemic?"

Flor had said what Bonnie wanted said.

"Oh, I know," said Flor's mother eagerly. "I remember! Oh, lambie, when you were small, the awful chopped raw liver mess you had to eat! You were anemic. Of course I remember now."

"It makes me tired," said Flor gently. "Then there's Doctor L., three times a week. That's tiring too. It just wears me out. And so, I lie down. August alone will be just wonderful. I'll lie down all the time. I'm *anemic*, Mama."

Bonnie's soft eager eyes were on her daughter. She would have cried at her, if she dared, Yes, tell me, make me believe this.

Now, that was the disarming thing about Flor. She could be so sensible, she could explain everything as though you were the nitwit. She could smile: "Don't *worry* about me," and you would think, Flor knows what she's doing. She's all right.

All the same, thought Bonnie, it was a pity that she was only twenty-six and had lost her looks.

Bob Harris had no division of purpose. He wanted Flor to go away from Paris for the next four weeks. Sometimes he said Cannes, because she liked the sea. He mentioned Deauville, but Bonnie pulled a long face. He knew there was more to it than getting through August, but that was all there was time for now. His father had arrived from New York. He was a mild old man, who had not wanted this marriage. He seemed to take up no space in the apartment, and he made everyone generous gifts. Bonnie tried to charm him, and failed. She tried to treat him like a joint parent, with foolish young people to consider, but that failed too. She gave up. She felt that disapproval of the match should be her own family's prerogative and that the Harrises were overstepping. The old man saw Flor, her silence, her absence, and believed she had a lover and that her pallor was owing to guilty thoughts. The young people had been married two years: it seemed to him a sad and wretched affair. There were no children and no talk of any. He thought, *I warned him*, but he held still: he did not want to cause the estrangement of his only son. His gentle sadness affected them all. He was thinly polite, and looked unwell. His skin had the bluish clarity of skimmed milk. Bonnie wanted to scream at him: I didn't want your son! She wondered why he felt he had to be so damned courtly. In her mind there was no social gap between a Jewish wine merchant and her ex-husband's old bootlegger of thirty years before.

Bonnie and her son-in-law were linked in one effort: keeping the old man from knowing the true state of affairs. Bonnie was always willing to unite when their common existence was threatened. She deplored the marriage and believed Flor might have made a better match, but most of the time she was grateful. She worshiped the Harris money: she would have washed all the Harris feet every day if that had been part of the deal. There had always been an unspoken, antagonistic agreement with Bob, which Flor had never understood. She never understood why Bob was nice to her mother. She guessed — that was at the start, when she was still curious and working things out — that it was Jewishness, respect for parents. But this was a subject from which he slid away. Evasion was seared into his personality. He had a characteristic sliding movement of head and body when conversation took a turn he didn't like. It was partly because of this that they had named him the Seal.

The façade they put up now was almost flawless: the old man may even have been deceived. In the effort, they were obliged to look at themselves, and these moments, near-horror, near-perfection, were unrehearsed. They dragged resisting Flor to parties, to restaurants, to the theater. At times Bob and Bonnie began to believe in the situation, and they would say, in amazement, "There, do you see how good life can be?" Flor seemed quite normal, except that she complained of being tired, but many women are like that. One day they made an excursion to Montparnasse: Bob bought pictures, and Bonnie had unearthed a young artist. She said he was Polish and full of genius. It was a bad outing: Bob was irritated because Bonnie had promised to help the young man without telling him first. The studio was like dozens more in Paris: there was a stove with last year's ashes, and the pictures he showed them were cold and stale. There was a flattering drawing of Bonnie tacked to the wall. The painter talked as if he owed his diction to an attentive study of old Charles Boyer films. He had a ripe-pear voice and a French accent.

"I don't like him," said Bob, when they were driving home. "He's nothing. He paints like a little girl. Anyway, he's a phony. What's that accent? He's just a New York boy."

"He has lived here for many years," said Bonnie, the bristling mother-bird.

"I may live here a lot longer but that won't change my voice," said Bob. "He's afraid. He's scared of being what he really is. If he talked naturally he wouldn't be Michel Colbert. Colbert. Colbert. What is that?"

"What is Harris?" said Bonnie, trembling.

Nothing was said, nothing was said about anything, and the silence beat about them like waves. The elevator in the building wasn't working again. Bonnie clutched at Flor as they climbed the stairs. "What have I gone and done?" she whispered heavily, pinching Flor's arm.

Flor had not been lying down a minute before her husband came in and slammed the door behind him. He stood over her and said, "Why the hell didn't you back me up?"

"I didn't listen," said Flor in terror. "I didn't speak."

"That's what I'm saying. What do you suppose my father thinks?"

He didn't go on with it. Too much had been taken away from him. He did not want to diminish what remained. Flor seemed frightened, looking up at him, curled on the bed like a child, and he was filled with pity for her and for them all. She had been dragged from her bed for the futile visit to the studio and now he had to drag her out again. She was a sick girl: he had to remember that. He sat on the bed with his back half turned and said gently, "We have to go out for dinner, you know?"

"Oh, no, no."

"It's my father and some of his friends," he said. "You know I have to be there. These people have invited us. Bonnie's coming." By this he meant that Bonnie understood the requirements of life.

"I'd rather not go."

He was so tired, yet he was someone who had never been tired. He thought, You shouldn't have to plead with your wife over such simple things. "It'll do you good," he said.

"I went to the studio," she said plaintively.

"People go two places in one day," he said. "It's not late. It's summer. It's still light outside. If you'd open those shutters you'd see." He had a fixed idea that she feared the dark.

Light and dark were outside the scope of her fears. She moved her head, unable to speak. He would have taken her hand only he never touched her now. In the spring, she had begun pleading with him to let her sleep. She had behaved like a prisoner roused for questioning. Tomorrow, she had promised, or in the morning. Any moment but now. He woke her one dawn and was humiliated at what they had become, remembering Cannes, the summer they had met. He couldn't discuss it. He never touched her again. He couldn't look at her now. Her hair, loose on the pillow, was a parody of Cannes. So were the shuttered windows.

Flor felt his presence. She had closed her eyes but held his image under the lids. He was half turned away. His back and the shape of his head were against the faint summer light that came in between the slats of the shutters. One hand was flat on the bed, and there was the memory of their hands side by side on the warm sand.

When he had moved his hand to cover hers, there remained the imprint of his palm, and, because they were both instinctively superstitious, they had brushed this mold away.

He said in such a miserable voice, "Are you really all that tired?" that she wanted to help him.

She said, "I've already told you. I'm afraid."

He had heard of her fear of cars but couldn't believe it. He had never been afraid: he was the circus seal. They had always clapped and approved. He tried to assemble some of the practical causes of fear. "Are you afraid of the next war? I mean, do you think about the bombs and all that?"

Flor moved her head on the pillow. "It's nothing like that. I don't think about the war. I'm used to the idea, like everyone else." She tried again. "Remember once when we were out walking, remember under the bridge, the boy kicking the man? The man was lying down."

"What's the good of thinking about that?" he said. "Somebody's kicking somebody else all the time. You can't make yourself responsible for everything."

"Why didn't the man at least get up? His eyes were open."

He had been afraid she would say, Why didn't we help him? The incident had seemed even when they were witnessing it far away and grotesque. When you live in a foreign country you learn to mind your own business. But all this reasoning was left in the air. He knew she was making a vertiginous effort to turn back on her journey out. He said something he hadn't thought of until now. It seemed irrefutable: "We don't know what the man had done to him first." Perhaps she accepted this; it caused a silence. "I'm glad you're talking to me," he said humbly, even though he felt she had put him in the wrong.

"I'm afraid of things like that," said Flor.

"Nobody's going to pull you under a bridge and kick you." He looked at her curiously, for she had used a false voice; not as Bonnie sometimes did, but as if someone were actually speaking for her.

"Sometimes when I want to speak," she said in the same way, "something comes between my thoughts and the words." She loathed herself at this moment. She believed she gave off a rank smell. She was the sick redhead; the dying, quivering fox. "It's only being anemic," she said wildly. "The blood doesn't reach the brain."

On an impulse stronger than pride he had already taken her hand. This hand was warm and dry and belonged to someone known. He had loved her: he tried to reconstruct their past, not sentimentally, but as a living structure of hair, skin, breath. This effort surpassed his imagination and was actually repugnant. It seemed unhealthy. Still, remembering, he said, "I do love you," but he was thinking of the hot, faded summer in Cannes, and the white walls of his shut-

tered room on a blazing afternoon, and coming
in with Flor from the beach. He saw the imprint
of his fingers on her brown shoulder; he thought
he tasted salt. Suddenly he felt as if he might
vomit. His mouth was flooded with saliva. He
thought, I'll go crazy with this. He was appalled
at the tenderness of the wound. He remembered
what it was to be sick with love.

"You'd better come out," he said. "It'll do you
good. You'll see there's nothing to be afraid of."
With these words he caused them to resume their
new roles: the tiresome wife, the patient husband.

He had never insisted so much before; but
too much had been taken away in his wife's retreat and he had been, without knowing it, building on what was left: money, and his own charm.
He could not stop charming people. The
concierge was minutes recovering from his greet-
ing every day. These elements — the importance
of business, his own attractive powers — pulled
away like the sea and left him stranded and without his wife.

Flor's crisis had passed. The sharp-muzzled
animal who inhabited her breast had gone to
sleep. She looked at her husband and saw that
whatever protected him had left him at that moment; he seemed pitiable and without confidence.
She might have said, Forgive me, or even, Help
me, and it might have been different between
them, if not better, but Bonnie came in. She

knocked and must have thought she heard an
answer. Neither Bob nor Flor heard clearly what
she said. The present rushed in with a clatter, for
Bonnie threw the shutters apart with an exclama-
tion of annoyance, and past love, that delicate
goblet, was shattered on the spot.

Bob stood beside Bonnie. Between them,
joined enemies again, they got Flor up and
out. "I shall never forgive you," said Flor; but
she rose, bathed, put up her hair. Their joint
feeling — her and Bob's — was one of relief:
there was no need to suffer too deeply after all.
No present horror equaled the potential suffering
of the past. Reliving the past, with full knowledge
of what was to come, was a test too strong for
their powers. It would have been too strong for
anyone; they were not magical; they were only
human beings.

Two days after this, on the fourth of August,
everyone except Flor went away. The cook and
the maid had already departed for Brittany, each
weighted with a full, shabby suitcase. Bob and
his father left by car in the morning. Bob was
hearty and rather vulgar and distrait, saying
goodbye. He patted Flor on the buttocks and
kissed her mouth. This took place on the street.
She had come down to see them loading the car
— just like any young woman seeing vacationers
off. She stood with her arms around her body, as
if the day were cold. The old man, now totally

convinced that Flor had a lover in Paris, did not look at her directly. In the afternoon, Bonnie took off from the Gare St. Lazare and Flor went there too. The station was so crowded that they had to fight their way to the train. Bonnie kept behaving as though it were all slick and usual and out of a page entitled "Doings of the International Smart Set": young Mrs. Robert Harris seeing her mother off for Deauville. Bonnie was beautifully dressed. She wore a public smile and gave her daughter a woman's kiss, embracing the air.

Flor saw the train out. She went home and got out of her clothes and into a nightgown covered with a pattern of butterflies. She had left a message for the cleaning woman, telling her not to come. She went from room to room and closed the shutters. Then she got into bed.

She slept without stirring until the next morning, when there was a ring at the door. Doris Fischer was there. She looked glossy and sunburned, and said she had caught a throat virus from the swimming pool in the Seine. She was hard, sunny reality; the opponent of dreams. She sat by Flor's bed and talked in disconnected sentences about people back in the States Flor had never seen. At noon, she went into the kitchen and heated soup, which they drank from cups. Then she went away. Flor lay still. She thought of the names of streets she had lived in and of hotel rooms in which she had spent the night. She leaned on her elbow and got her notebook from the table nearby. This was an invalid's gesture: the pale hand fretfully clutching the magic object. There were no blank pages. She had used them all in the letter. She looked at a page on which she had written this:

Maids dancing in Aunt Dottie Fairlie's kitchen.

Father Doyle: If you look in the mirror too much you will see the devil.

Granny's gardener

B. H.: The only thing I like about Christ is when he raised the little girl from the dead and said she should be given something to eat.

She turned the pages. None of these fragments led back or forward to anything and many called up no precise image at all. There was nothing to add, even if there had been space. The major discovery had been made that July afternoon before the Café de la Paix, and the words, "it was always this way," were the full solution. Even Dr. Linnetti would have conceded that.

She could not sleep unless her box of sleeping tablets was within sight. She placed the round box on the notebook and slept again. The next day, Doris returned. She sat by Flor's bed because Bonnie had gone and there was no one else. The traffic outside was muffled to a rustling of tissue paper, the room green-dark.

"What are those pill things for?" Doris said.

"Pains," said Flor. "My teeth ache. It's something that only happens in France and it's called *rage de dents*."

"I've got good big teeth and I've never had a filling," said Doris, showing them. "That's from the German side. I'm half Irish, half German. Florence, why don't you get up? If you lie there thinking you're sick you'll *get* sick."

"I know perfectly well I'm not sick," said Flor.

Doris thought she was on to something. "You know, of course," she said, fixing Flor sternly, "that this is a retreat from life."

For the first time since Doris had known her, Flor laughed. She laughed until Doris joined in too, good-natured, but slightly vexed, for she guessed she was being made fun of.

"Don't worry about me," said Flor, as lucidly as you pleased. "I'm a Victorian heroine."

"The trouble is," Doris said, "you've never had to face a concrete problem. Like mine. Like . . ." and she was away, divulging the affairs she had only hinted at until now. Her husband had left her, but only for the summer. He intended to return, and she knew she would take him back, and that should have been the end of it. That was the story, but Doris couldn't leave it alone. Behind the situation struggled memories and impulses she could neither relate nor control. Trying to bring order through speech, she sat by Flor's bed and told her about their life in New York, which had been so different. Names emerged: Beth and Howard, Peter and Jan, Bernie and Madge, Lina, who was brilliant, and Wolff and Louis, who always came to see them

on Sundays, and lived in a stable or garage or
something like that. They were prudently left-
wing, and on speaking terms with a number of
jazz musicians. They had among their friends
Chinese, Javanese, Peruvians, and Syrians. They
had a wonderful life. Then this year abroad things
had happened and her husband, filming a docu-
mentary for television, had met a woman study-
ing Egyptian at the Ecole du Louvre. "Don't
laugh," said Doris miserably to Flor, who was
not laughing at all.

Why did these things happen? Why was Doris
alone in Paris, who had never been alone in her
life? Why weren't they still in college or still in
New York? Why was she nearly thirty and in a
foreign place and everything a mess? "You tell
me," Doris demanded.

Flor had no replies. She lay on the bed, in a
butterfly-covered nightgown, and her dreams
were broken by Doris's ring at the door. Doris
occupied the chair beside her bed as if she had a
right to it. She came every day. She opened cans
of soup in the kitchen and she never washed the
saucepan or the cups. She took clean dishes from
the cupboard each time, and it was like the Mad
Tea Party; although even there, eventually, it
must have become impossible to move along.
The dishes here would finally reach an end too,
and she would have to do something — go home,
or follow her husband, whether he wanted her
around or not, or stay here and wash cups. Flor

was not making the division between days and nights clearly, but she knew that Doris came most frequently in the afternoon. She told Flor that she woke up fairly optimistically each day, but that the afternoon was a desert and she couldn't cross it alone.

Then a disaster occurred: Flor's sleeping tablets disappeared. She took the bed apart and rolled back the carpet. Doris helped, unexpectedly silent. It was a disaster because without the pills in the room she was unable to sleep. Her desire for sleep and dreams took the shape of a boat. Every day it pulled away from shore but was forced to return. She had left the doorkey under the mat so that Doris could come in when she wanted, after a warning ring. She got up early one day and took the key inside. She heard a ring and didn't answer. The ring was repeated, and Doris knocked as well, but Flor lay still, her eyes closed. Once the imperative ring surprised her in the kitchen, where she was distractedly looking around for something to eat. There were empty cans everywhere, which Doris had opened for her, and dirty cups, and a spilled box of crackers. She found cornflakes and some sour milk in a jug and a sticky packet of dates. In a store cupboard there were more tins. She opened a tin of mushrooms and ate them with her fingers and went back to bed. This scene had the air of a robbery. It was midday, but the light was on; the kitchen was shuttered, like every other room.

Flor's quest for food was stealthy and uncertain, partly because the kitchen was not her province and she seldom entered it. When Doris rang, she stood frozen, in her nightgown, her head thrown back, her heart beating in hard, painful, slow thumps. She had a transient fear that Doris possessed a miraculous key and could come in whenever she wanted to. She felt the warmth and weight of her thick hair. Her neck was damp with fear.

The ringing stopped. That afternoon she slept and half slept and had her first real dream, which was of floating, sailing, going away. It was pleassant, brightly lit, and faintly erotic. There emerged the face of a Russian she and her mother had once talked to in a hotel. She remembered that in the presence of a whirlwind you defied Satan and made the sign of the cross. She opened her eyes with interest and wonder. She had followed someone exorcising a number of rooms. She was not in the least frightened, but she was half out of bed.

The building was empty now. She heard the concierge cleaning on the stairs. In the daytime there was light through the shutters. She was happiest at night, but her plans were upset by the loss of the pills. Once her husband telephoned and she replied and spoke quite sensibly, although she could not remember afterward what she had said. She turned her room upside down again, but the pills were gone. Well, the pills might turn up. There were other things to be done: cupboards to be shut, drawers tidied, stockings put away. She knew she would be unable to lie in peace until everything was settled, and August was wearing away. Every day she did one useful thing. There were the gold sandals Bonnie wanted repaired: she had left them on a chest in the hall so that Flor would see them on her way out. These sandals did not belong in the hall. The need to find a place for the broken sandals drove her out of bed one afternoon. She carried the sandals all around the flat, from shuttered room to room. There was no sound from the street. In her mother's bedroom she forgot why she had come. She let the sandals fall on a chair; that was how Bonnie found them, one on the chair, one on the floor, with its severed strap like a snapped twig some inches away.

Once she had told Dr. Linnetti that her husband was her mother's lover. She had described in a composed voice the scene of discovery: he came home very late and instead of going into his own room went into Bonnie's. She knew it was he, for she knew his step, and the words this man used were his. She heard her mother whisper and her mother laugh. "Then," said Flor, "he tried to come to me, but I wouldn't have it. No, never again." A month later she said, "That wasn't true, about Bob and my mother." "I know," said Dr. Linnetti.

"How do you know?" said Flor, trembling, in Bonnie's room. "How do you know?"

She saw herself in a long glass, in the long loose butterfly-covered nightdress. She looked like a pale rose model in a fashion magazine, neat, sweet, a porcelain figure, intended to suggest that it suffices to be desirable — that the dream of love is preferable to love in life.

"You might cut your hair," said Bonnie.

"Yes," said Flor. "You'd love that, wouldn't you?"

Bonnie's windows were closed and the oyster-silk fringed curtains pulled together. But still light came into the room, the milky light of August, in which Flor, the dreamer, floated like a seed. Bonnie had not entirely removed herself to Deauville, for her scent clouded the room — the cat's-fur Spanish-servant-girl scent she bought for herself in expensive bottles. Flor moved out of the range of the looking glass and could no longer be witnessed. She opened a mothproof closet and looked at dresses without touching them. She looked at chocolates from Holland in a tin box. She looked desultorily for her pills. She forgot what she was doing here and returned to bed.

She knew that time was going by and the city was emptying, and still she hadn't achieved the dreams she desired. One day she opened the shutters of her bedroom and the summer afternoon fell on her white face and tangled hair. There was the feeling of summer ending; it had reached its peak and could only wane. Nostalgia came into the room — for the past, for the wan-

ing of a day, for a shadow through a blind, for
the fear of autumn. It was a season not so much
ending as already used up, like a love too long
discussed or a desire deferred. An accumula-
tion of shadows and seasons ending led back to
some scene: maids dancing in Aunt Dottie's
kitchen? She held the shutters out and apart
with both hands, frozen, as if calling for aid.
None came, and she drew in her thin arms and
brought the shutters to.

She was interrupted by the concierge, who
brought letters, and said, "Are you still not better?" She left unopened the letters from her husband because she knew he was not saying anything to her. She opened all the letters from Dr.
Linnetti, those addressed to herself, and to her
mother and her husband as well. She had long
ago intercepted and destroyed the first letter to
Bob: "Her hostility to me was expected . . ."
(Oh, she had no pride!) "but she is in need of
help." She gave the name of another doctor
and said that this doctor was a man.

Flor had no time for doctors. She had to finish sewing a dress. She became brisk and busy
and decided to make one dress of two, fastening
the bodice of one to the skirt of the other. For
two days she sewed this dress and in one took it
apart. She unpicked it stitch by stitch and left
the pieces on the floor. She was quite happy,
humming, remembering the names of songs.
She wandered into Bonnie's room. The moth-

proof closet was open, as she had left it. She took down a heavy brocaded cocktail dress and with Bonnie's nail scissors began picking the seams apart. There was a snowdrift of threads on the parquet. The carpet had been taken away. When she went back to bed, she could sleep, but she was sleeping fitfully. There were no dreams. It was days since she had looked into the notebook. The plants were dying without water and the kitchen light left burning night and day. For the first time in her memory she was frightened of the dark. When she awoke at night it was to a whirling world of darkness and she was frightened. Then she remembered that Bonnie had taken the prescription for the sleeping tablets and she found it easily in the jewel case, lower tray.

She dressed and went down the stairs, trembling like an invalid, holding the curving rail. The concierge put letters in her hand, saying something Flor could not hear. She went out into the empty city. The quarter was completely deserted and there was no one in the park. She saw from the fit of her dress that she had lost pounds. It was the last Sunday of August, and every pharmacy she came to was closed. The air was heavy and still. There was no variation in the color of the sky. It might have been nine in the morning or four in the afternoon. The city had perished and everyone in it died or gone away: she had perceived this on a July day, crossing the Pont Neuf. It was more than a fancy, it was true. The ruin was incomplete. The streets lacked the crevices in which would appear the hellebore, the lizards, the poppies, the ivy, the nesting birds. High up at one of the windows was a red geranium, the only color on the gray street. It flowered, abandoned, on its ledge, like the poppies and the cowslips whose seeds are carried by the wind and by birds to the highest point of a ruin.

There were no cars. She was able to cross every street. The only possible menace came from one of the letters the concierge had put in her hand. She came to a café filled with people, huddled together on the quiet avenue. She sat down and opened the letter. It was nearly impossible to read, but one sentence emerged with clarity: "I am writing to Dr. Linnetti and telling her I think it is *unprofessional* to say the least," and one page she read from the start to the end: "I want this man to see you. It is something entirely new. Everything we think of as mental comes from a different part of your body and it is only a matter of getting all these different parts under control. You have always been so strong-minded darling it should be easy for you. It is *not* that Swiss and *not* that Russian but someone quite new, and he had helped thousands. When he came into the room darling we all got to our feet, it was as if some unseen force was pulling us, and although he said very little every word counted. He is most attractive darling but of course above and outside all that. I asked him what he thought of The Box and he said it was all nonsense so you see darling he isn't a fake. When I explained about The Box and how you put a drop of blood on a bit of blotting paper and The Box makes a diagnosis he was absolutely horrified so you see love he isn't a fake at all. I remember how you were so scornful when The Box diagnosed my liver trouble (that all the doctors thought was heart) so it must be an assurance for you that he doesn't believe in it too. Darling he was so interested in hearing about you. I am going to ask Dr. Linnetti why you must pay even if away and why you must have sessions in August. He is coming to Paris and you must meet. He doesn't have fees or fixed hours, you come when you need him and you give what you can to his Foundation."

She became conscious of a sound, as a sound in the fabric of a dream. Florence looked away from Bonnie's letter and saw that this sound was real. At one of the café tables, a laughing couple were pretending to give a child away to a policeman. The policeman played his role well, swinging his cape, pretending to be fierce. "She is very naughty," said the mother, when she could stop laughing enough to speak, "and I think prison is the best solution." All the people in the café laughed, except Flor. They opened their mouths in the same way, eyes fixed on the policeman and the child. The child cried out that it would be good, now, but everyone was too excited to pay attention. The child gave one more promise and suddenly went white and stiff in the policeman's grasp. He gave her back to her parents, who sat her on a chair. "She'll be good now," the policeman said.

The closed face of Paris relaxed. This was Paris: this was France. Oh, it was not only France. Her mother's mother's gardener had broken the necks of goldfinches. "If you tell you saw, you'll get hit by lightning," he had said.

"It's because of things like that," said Florence earnestly, retracing her steps home, "I'm not afraid of bombs."

She unlocked the empty apartment and the element she recognized and needed but that had evaded her until now rushed forward to meet her, and she knew it was still August, that she was still alone, and there was still time. "I only need a long sleep," she said to the empty air. The unopened letters from Bob she put on the chest in the hall. Her advancing foot kicked something along and it was a trodden, folded letter that had been pushed under the door. It was dirty and had been walked on and was greasy with city dust. She carried this letter — three sheets folded one over the other — around the flat. She closed all the doors except the door of the kitchen and the door of her bedroom. The passage was a funnel. Her sleep had been a longer and longer journey away from shore. She lay down on the bed, having been careful to remove her shoes. The letter spoke to her in peaked handwriting. She had no idea who it was from.

"I have stupid ideas," said this pointed hand, "and you are right to have nothing to do with me. You are so beautiful and clever." It groveled on like this for lines. Who is the writer of this letter? Her husband loves her but has gone away with another woman. "The girl knows I know, and it doesn't work, we are all unhappy, he has his work, and I can't just make a life of my own as he suggests. I thought you would help me but why should you? You are right not to let anyone hang on your skirts. The important thing is that I have made a decision, because I understood when you locked me out that what is needed is not slow suffering or hanging on to someone else, but a solution. I went out on the street that day and wanted to die because you had locked me out and I realized that there was a solution for me and the solution was a decision and so now I am going home. I am not going *away* but going *home*. He can follow, or he can stay, or he can do what he likes, but I have made a decision and I have cabled my father and he is cabling the money and I am going home. I'm leaving on the sixteenth and I'll wait for you every evening, come down if you want to say goodbye. I won't bother you again. All I want to tell you is I hid your sleeping pills and now I know I had no right to do that, because every person's decision is his own. I know I was silly because you're young and pretty and have everything to live for and you wouldn't do what I was afraid you would. I can't even write the word. You may have been wanting those pills and I'm sorry. They're in the kitchen, inside the white tin box with "Recipes" written on it. Don't be angry with my interference and please Florence come and say goodbye. Florence, another thing. Everybody makes someone else pay for something, I don't know why. If you are as awful to your mother as she says you are, you are making her pay, but then, Florence, your mother could turn around and say, "Yes, but look at my parents," and they could have done and said the same thing, so you see how pointless it is to fix any blame. I think my husband is making me pay, but I don't know what for or why. Everyone does it. We all pay and pay for someone else's troubles. All children eventually make their parents pay, and pay, and pay. That's the way I see it now, although I may come to change my mind when I have children of my own. Florence, come once and say goodbye."

She had no time and no desire to say, They have paid. At the edge of the sea, the Fox departed. She saw the animal head breaking the water and the fan-shaped ripples diminishing against the shore. She turned her back and left the sea behind. At last she was going in the right direction. She rode Chief, her pony, between an alley of trees. Chief was a devil: he daren't bolt, or rear, but he sometimes tried to catch her leg against a tree. Nearby somebody smiled. She held herself straight. She was perfect. Everyone smiled now. Everyone was pleased. She emerged in triumph from the little wood and came off Chief, her pony, and into her father's arms.

III
III
III
III
III
III

DREAMS OF CHAOS were Wishart's meat; he was proud of their diversity, and of his trick of emerging from mortal danger unscathed. The slightest change in pace provoked a nightmare, so that it was no surprise to him when, falling asleep in his compartment a few seconds before the train arrived at Cannes, he had a dream that lasted hours about a sinking ferryboat outside the harbor. Millions of limp victims bowled elegantly out of the waves, water draining from their skin and hair. There were a few survivors, but neither they, nor the officials who had arrived in great haste, knew what to do next. They milled about on the rocky shore looking unsteady and pale. Even the victims seemed more drunk than dead. Out of this deplorable confusion Wishart strode, suitably dressed in a bathing costume. He shook his head gravely, but without pity, and moved out and away. As usual, he had foreseen the disaster, but failed to give warning. Explanations unrolled in his sleeping mind: "I never interfere. It was up to them to ask me. They knew I was there." His triumph was only on a moral level. He had no physical vanity at all. He observed with detachment his drooping bathing trunks, his skinny legs, his white freckled hands, his brushed-out fringe of graying hair. None of it humbled him. His body had never given him much concern.

He was pleased with the dream. No one was gifted with a subconscious quite like Wishart's, tirelessly creative, producing without effort any number of small visual poems in excellent taste. This one might have been a ballet, he decided, or, better still, because of the black and white groupings and the unmoving light, an experimental film, to be called simply and cryptically "Wishart's Dream." He could manipulate this name without conceit, for it was not his own. That is, it was not the name that had been gummed onto his personality some forty years before without thought or care: "Wishart" was selected, like all the pieces of his fabricated life. Even the way he looked was contrived, and if, on bad days, he resembled nothing so much as a failed actor afflicted with dreams, he accepted this resemblance, putting it down to artistic fatigue. He did not consider himself a failed anything. Success can only be measured in terms of distance traveled, and, in Wishart's case, it had been a long flight. No wonder he looked wearing, he would think, seeing his sagged face in the glass. He had lived one of society's most grueling roles, the escape from an English slum. He had been the sturdy boy with vision in his eyes — that picked-over literary bone. "Scramble, scrape, and scholarship" should have been written on his brow, and, inside balloons emerging from his brain, "a talent for accents," and "a genius for kicking the past from his shoes." He had other attributes, of course, but it wasn't necessary to crowd the image.

Wishart's journey was by no means unusual, but he had managed it better than nearly anyone. Most scramblers and scrapers take the inherited structure with them, patching and camouflaging as they can, but Wishart had knocked his flat. He had given himself a name, parents, and a class of his choice. Now, at forty-two, he passed as an English gentleman in America, where he lived, and as an awfully decent American when he went to England. He had little sense of humor where his affairs were concerned, no more than a designer of comic postcards can be funny about his art, but he did sometimes see it as a joke on life that the quirks and crotchets with which he was laced had grown out of an imaginary past. Having given himself a tall squire of a father, who adored horses and dogs, Wishart first simulated, then genuinely felt, a disgust and terror of the beasts. The phantom parent was a brandy-

swiller: Wishart wouldn't drink. Indeed, as created by his equally phantom son, the squire was
impeccably *bien élevé* but rather a brute: he had
not been wholly kind to Wishart, the moody,
spindly boy. Wishart often regretted that he
would never overtake the mighty Pa, in manli-
ness, that is; he had already outrun him in brains.
He said this to friends. The friends, seeing a
clear-cut case, urged him to free himself from
the shadow of Pa, and Wishart would promise to
try. For a time he would try, as if the squire in
his great boots had existed, as if there had been
a moony Wishart in the garret reading Keats.
Now that was surely a joke, or might have been,
if only there had been someone to share it with.
But Wishart had no witnesses. The only person
out of the real past he remembered without disgust was a sister, Glad, who had become a servant at eleven and had taught him how to eat with
a knife and fork. The joke was airtight; Wishart
was safe. He had an innocent faith that the past,
severed from him, could not persist in a life of
its own.

At the beginning, in the old days, before he
had been intelligent enough to settle for the
squire and had hinted at something grand, he
had often been the victim of sudden frights, when
an element, hidden and threatening, had bub-
bled under his feet, and he had felt the soles
of his shoes growing warm, so thin, so friable
was the crust of his poor world. Nowadays, he
moved in a gassy atmosphere of goodwill and

feigned successes. He seemed invulnerable. Strangers meeting him for the first time often thought he must be celebrated, and wondered why they had never heard of him before. There was no earthly reason for anyone's having done so: he was a teacher of dramatics in a preparatory school, and once this was revealed, and the shoddiness of the school established, it required Wishart's most hypnotic gifts, his most persuasive monologue, to maintain the effect of his person. As a teacher he was barely adequate, and, if he had been an American, his American school would never have kept him. His British personality — sardonic, dry — replaced ability or even ambition. Privately, he believed he was wasted in a world of men and boys, and had never bothered giving them the full blaze of his Wishart creation; he saved it for a world of women. Like many spiteful, snobbish, fussy men, or a certain type of murderer, Wishart chose his friends among middle-aged solitary women. These women were widowed or divorced, and lived in places Wishart liked to visit. Every summer, then, shedding his working life, a shining Wishart took off for Europe, where he spent the summer alighting here and there, depending on the topography of his invitations. He lived on his hostesses, without shame. He was needed and liked: his invitations began arriving at Christmas. He knew that women who will fret over wasting the last bit of soap, or a torn postage stamp, or an unused return ticket, will pay without a murmur for the company of a man. Wishart was no hired companion — carrier of coats, fetcher of aspirin, walker of dachshunds. He considered it enough to be there, supplying gossip and a listening ear. Often Wishart's friends took it for granted he was homosexual, which was all to the good. He was the chosen minstrel, the symbolic male, who would never cause "trouble." He knew this: it was a galling thought. But he had never managed to correct it. He was much too busy keeping his personality in place so that it wouldn't slip or collapse even in his dreams. He had never found time for such an enervating activity as proving his virility, which might not only divert the movement of his ambitions, but could, indeed, take up an entire life. He had what he wanted, and it was enough: he had never desired a fleet of oil tankers. It sufficed him to be accepted here and there. His life would probably have been easier if he had not felt obliged to be something special on two continents, but he was compelled to return to England now, every year, and make them accept him. They accepted him as an American, but that was part of the buried joke. Sometimes he ventured a few risks, such as "we were most frightfully poor when I was a child," but he knew he still hadn't achieved the right tone. The most successful impostures are based on truth, but how poor is poor, and how closely should he approach this burning fact? (Particularly in England, where the whole structure could collapse for the sake of a vowel.) These were the trials that beset poor Wishart, and sometimes caused him to look like a failed actor who has had a bad dream.

He got down from the train, holding his artfully bashed-up suitcase, and saw, in the shadow of the station, Mrs. Bonnie McCarthy, his best American friend. She was his relay in the south of France, a point of refreshment between the nasal sculptress in London who had been his first hostess of the season and a Mrs. Sebastian in Venice. It would have been sweet for Wishart at this moment if he could have summoned an observer from the past, a control to establish how far he had come. Supposing one of the populated waves of his dream had deposited sister Glad on shore? He saw her in cap and apron, a dour little girl, watching him being greeted by this woman who would not as much as have spat in their direction if she had known them in the old days. At this thought he felt a faint stir, like the rumor of an earthquake some distance away. But he knew he had nothing to fear and that the source of terror was in his own mistakes. It had been a mistake to remember Glad.

"Wishart," his friend said gravely, without breaking her pose. Leaning on a furled peach-colored parasol, she gave the appearance of living a minute of calm in the middle of a hounding

social existence. She turned to him the soft,
myopic eyes that had been admired when she
was a girl. Her hair was cut in the year's fashion,
like an inverted peony, and she seemed to Wishart beautifully dressed. She might have been
waiting for something beyond Wishart and better than a friend, some elegant paradise he could
not imagine, let alone attain. His admiration of
her (charm, wealth, aspirations) flowed easily
into admiration of himself: after all, he had
achieved this friend. Almost tearful with self-
felicitation, he forgot how often he and Bonnie
had quarreled in the past. Their kiss of friendship outside the station was real.

"Did you get my telegram?" he said, beginning the nervous remarks that preceded and followed all his journeys. He had prepared his
coming with a message: "Very depressed London like old blotting paper longing for sea sun
you." This wire he had signed Baronne Putbus.
(There was no address, so that Bonnie was unable to return a killing answer she would have
signed Lysistrata.)

"I died," Bonnie said, looking with grave liquid eyes. "I just simply perished." After the
nasal sculptress and her educated vowels, Bonnie's slight drawl fell gently on his ear. She continued to look at him gaily, without making a
move, and he began to feel some unease in the
face of so much bright expectancy. He suddenly
thought, Good God, has she fallen in love? add-

ing in much smaller print, with me? Accidents
of that sort had happened in the past. Now,
Wishart's personality being an object he used
with discretion, when he was doubtful, or simply
at rest, he became a sort of mirror. Reflected in
this mirror, Bonnie McCarthy saw that she was
still pretty and smart. Dear darling Wishart!
He also gave back her own air of waiting. Each
thought that the other must have received a piece
of wonderful news. Wishart was not envious;
he knew that the backwash of someone else's fortune can be very pleasant indeed, and he waited
for Bonnie's good tidings to be revealed. Perhaps she had rented a villa, so that he would not
have to stay in a hotel. That would be nice.

"The hotel isn't far," Bonnie said, stirring them
into motion at last. "Do you want to walk a little,
Wishart? It's a lovely, lovely day."

No villa, then; and if the hotel was nearby, no
sense paying a porter. Carrying his suitcase, he
followed her through the station and into the
sudden heat of the Mediterranean day. Later,
he would hate these streets, and the milling,
sweating, sunburned crowd; he would hurry past
the sour-milk smelling cafés with his hand over
his nose. But now, at first sight, Cannes looked
as it had sounded when he said the word in London, a composition in clear chalk colors, blue,
yellow, white. Everything was intensely shaded
or intensely bright, hard and yellow on the
streets, or dark as velvet inside the bars. Bonnie

seemed to be leading him somewhere. He supposed it had to do with her surprise.

"I hope you aren't cross because Florence isn't here," Bonnie said. "She was perishing to meet your train, but the poor baby had something in her eye. A grain of sand. She had to go to an oculist to have it taken out. You'll love seeing her now, Wishart. She's getting a style, you know? Everyone notices her. Somebody said to me on the beach — a total stranger — somebody said, Your daughter is like a Tanagra."

"Of which there are so many fakes."

Like many people who are too much concentrated on their own persons, Wishart sometimes believed he was invisible and could not be heard. He did not have a great opinion of his friend's intelligence, and may have thought that a slight obtuseness also affected her hearing. It was insensitive of her to mention Flor, now, just when Wishart was feeling so well. From the beginning, their friendship had been marred by the existence of Bonnie's daughter, a spoiled, sulky girl he had vainly tried to admire. He remembered her as a preener and head-tosser — that long tail of carrot hair! There was a wounding memory of her posturing on a beach and looking as though she had bitten a lemon every time Wishart opened his mouth. She had a jerky, resentful way of speaking and a detestable American voice. Wishart was an amusing mimic, and would have sacrificed any personality save his

own for the sake of a story. Re-created by Wishart, Bonnie emerged sounding like Zasu Pitts.
"And the daughter," he would say. "When she
parts those perfect lips to speak. Oh!" And he
would close his eyes in remembered pain. "But
then she *is* perfect. Why should Aphrodite ut-
ter?" This way of going on was one of his few
errors. He was not sure of his ground, had it all
at second hand. Even as a pose it was out of date.

"There are literally millions of men chasing
Flor," Bonnie said. "I've never seen anything
like it. Every time we go to the beach or the
casino . . ."

He realized with boredom — boredom that
was like having a dry biscuit stuffed in one's
mouth — that they were going to talk about
Venus-Flor. "She worships me," Bonnie used to
tell him. "That girl simply worships me." But
as far as Wishart could tell, it had always been
Flor on the altar with Mama at her feet.

"I'm surprised she hasn't offered you a son-
in-law," he said, knowing that this praise of Flor
was leading up to a complaint. "But I suppose
she is still too young."

"Oh, she isn't," Bonnie cried, standing still.
"Wishart, that girl is twenty-four. I don't know
what men want from women now. I don't even
know what Flor wants. We've been here since
the tenth of June, and do you know what she's
picked up? A teeny little fellow from Turkey.
I swear, he's not five three. When we go out, the

three of us, I could die. I don't understand it,
why she only likes the wrong kind. Only likes,
did I say? I should have said only *attracts*.
They're awful. They don't even propose. She
hasn't even got the satisfaction of turning them
down. I don't understand it and that's all I can
say. Why, I had literally hundreds of proposals,
and not from little Turkeys. I stuck to my own
kind."

He wanted to say, Yes, but you were among
your own kind. The girl is a floater, like me. He
sensed that Bonnie's disappointment in what she
called her own kind had affected her desires for
Flor. Her own kind had betrayed her; she had
told him so. That was why she lived in Europe.
Outside her own kind was a vast population of
men in suspenders standing up to carve the Sunday roast. That took care of Americans. They
walked on, slowly. A store window they passed
revealed the drawn, dried expression that added
years to Wishart's age but removed him from
competition and torment. He found time to admire the image, and was further comforted by
Bonnie's next, astonishing words:

"Someone like you, Wishart, would be good
for Flor. I mean someone older, a person I can
trust. You know what I mean, an Englishman
who's been in America, who's had the best of
both."

He knew that she could not be proposing him
as a husband for Florence, but he could have

loved her forever for the confirmation of the gentleman he had glimpsed in the window, the sardonic Englishman in America, the awfully decent American in England. He slipped his hand under her elbow; it was almost a caress. They reached the Croisette, crossed over to the sea side, and Bonnie put up her parasol. Wishart's ballooning good humor hung suspended as he looked down at the beaches, the larvae bodies, the rows of chairs. Every beach carried its own social stamp, as distinct as the strings of greasy flags, the raked, pullulating sand, the squalid little bar that marked the so-called students' beach, and the mauve and yellow awnings, the plastic mattresses of the beach that was a point of reunion for Parisian homosexuals. Wishart's gaze, uninterested, was about to slide over this beach when Bonnie arrested him by saying, "This is where we bathe, Wishart, dear." He turned his head so suddenly that her parasol hit him in the eye, which made him think of her falsehood about Flor and grain of sand. He looked with real suspicion now at the sand, probably treacherous with broken bottles, and at the sea, which, though blue and sparkling, was probably full of germs. Even the sky was violated: across the face of it an airplane was writing the name of a drink.

Bonnie has fallen into that one, he thought: Queen Bee of a pansy court.

"Oh, my sweet heaven," Bonnie said, unaware

of Wishart's busy brain. She stood still, clutching Wishart by the arm, and said it again: "Sweet heaven. Well, there she is. There's Flor. But that's not the Turk from Turkey. Now, Wishart, her mother is to have a treat. She's got a new one. Oh my sweet heaven Wishart where does she find them?"

"I expect she meets them in trains."

From that distance he could admire Bonnie's girl, thin and motionless, with brown skin and dark red hair. She leaned on the low wall, looking down at the sea, braced on her arms, as tense as if this decision over a beach was to decide the course of her life.

"She does have extraordinary coloring," he said, as generously as he could.

"She gets it from me," said Bonnie, shortly, as if she had never noticed her own hair was brown.

The man with Florence was stocky and dark. He wore sneakers, tartan swimming trunks of ample cut, a gold waterproof watch, a gold medal on a chain, and a Swedish university cap some sizes too small. He carried a net bag full of diving equipment. His chest was bare.

"Well, I don't know," Bonnie said. "I just don't know."

By a common silent decision the two rejected the beach and turned and came toward Bonnie. They gave an impression as harsh and unpoetical as the day. The sun had burned all expression from their faces, smooth brown masks in which

their eyes, his brown, hers green, shone like colored glass. Even though he had never dared
allow himself close relations, Wishart was aware
of their existence to a high degree. He could de-
tect an intimate situation from a glance, or a
quality of silence. It was one more of his gifts,
but he could have been happier without it.
Pushed by forces he had not summoned or in-
vented, he had at these moments a victim's face
— puzzled, wounded, bloodless, coarse. The gap
between the two couples closed. Bonnie had
taken on a dreamy, vacant air; she was not planning to help.

"This is Bob Harris," Florence said. "He's
from New York."

"I guessed that," Bonnie said.

It was plain to Wishart that the new man, now
sincerely shaking hands all around, had no idea
that Mrs. McCarthy might want to demolish him.
Perhaps it seemed suitable, almost proper, that
he should meet Flor's mother now. Wishart's
anguished guess had been in order: after days
of what had seemed to Bob interminable pursuit,
Florence had come to his room. He stayed in
one of the sugary palaces on the Croisette: the
room was too noisy, too bright, and it was Flor,
in the end, who had seemed most at ease, adjusting the blind so that slats of shade covered
the walls, placing her clothes neatly on a chair.
She seemed to him exclusive, a prize, even
though the evidence was that they were both

summer rats. He had met her in a café one afternoon. He saw his own shadow on her table and
himself, furtive, ratlike, looking for trouble. But
he was already forgetting this, and his slight disappointment in her, and in the untender afternoon. He was forming an evasive figure who was
only partly Flor; he remembered a half-darkened
room and a secret relation on another level of the
day. He noticed that Flor kissed her mother anx-
iously, as if they had been parted for days, or
as though he had taken Flor to another country.
The affection between the two women pleased
him. His own mother, having died, had elevated
the notion of motherhood. He liked people who
got on with their parents and suspected those
who did not.

Wishart permitted Bob to pump his hand up
and down, as if to show that he recognized good
manners when he saw them. Flor's sullen "Hullo
Wishart" had been worse than a snub. He decided that Bob was no problem where he was
concerned: his shrewdness was not the variety
likely to threaten Wishart, and he would take up
Flor's time, leaving Bonnie free to listen to Wishart's chat. He did not desire Bonnie to himself as
a lover might, but he did want to get on with his
anecdotes without continual interruptions.

Every day after that the four met on Bonnie's
beach and lunched in a restaurant Bonnie liked.
If Wishart had disapproved of the beach, it was
nothing to his opinion of the restaurant, which

was full of Bonnie's new friends. Wine — Algerian pink — came out of a barrel, there were paper flags stuck in the butter, the waiters were insolent and barefoot, the menu written on a slate and full of obscene puns. Everyone knew everyone, and Wishart could have murdered Bonnie. He was appalled at her thinking he could possibly like the place, but remembered that her attitude was the result of years of neuter camaraderie. It didn't matter: on the tenth of July he was expected in Venice. It was not a pattern of life.

It seemed to Wishart that Bonnie was becoming silly with age. She had developed a piercing laugh, and the affected drawl was becoming real. Her baiting of Bob Harris was too direct to be funny, and her antagonism was forming a bond between them — the last thing on earth she wanted. Bob had the habit of many Americans of constantly repeating the name of the person he was talking to. Bonnie retaliated by calling him Bob Harris in full, every time she spoke to him, and this, combined with her slightly artificial voice, made him ask, "Is that a southern accent you've got, Mrs. McCarthy?"

"Well, it just might be, Bob Harris," Bonnie cried, putting one on. But it was a movie accent; she did it badly, and it got on Wishart's nerves. "Well, that's a nice breeze that's just come up," she would say, trailing the vowels. "We're certainly a nice little party, aren't we? It's nice

being four." Nice being four? Nice for Wishart,
the adored, the sought-after, Europe's trouba-
dour? He closed his eyes and thought of Mrs.
Sebastian, Venice, shuttered room, green canals.
Then Florence burst out with something. Only
Wishart guessed that these cheeky outbursts, fit
for a child of twelve, were innocent attempts to
converse. Because of the way her mother had
dragged her around, because she had never been
part of a fixed society, she didn't know how people talked; she had none of the coins of light exchange. She said in an excited voice, "The Fox,
the Ape, the Bumblebee, were all at odds, being
three, and then the Goose came out the door, and
stayed the odds by making four. We're like that.
Mama's a lovely bumblebee and I'm fox-col-
ored." This left Wishart the vexing choice between being a goose and an ape, and he was the
more distressed to hear Bob say placidly that
it wasn't the first time he had been called a big
ape. All at once it seemed to him preferable to
be an ape than a goose.

"Have you got many friends in Paris, Bob Harris?" said Bonnie, as if she hadn't seen Wishart's
face pucker and shrink.

"Last year I had to send out one hundred and
sixty-nine Christmas cards," said Bob simply. "I
don't mean cards for the firm."

"The Bambino of the Eiffel Tower? Something
real Parisian?" Even as Bonnie was bringing this
out Wishart knew it was wrong. Bob looked

down, with a smile. He seemed to feel sorry for
Mrs. McCarthy, who didn't know about the cards
people sent now, nondenominational, either
funny or artistic, depending on your friends.

Alone with Wishart, Bonnie was the person
he liked. When they laughed together on the
beach it was like the old days when she had
seemed so superior, enchanting, and bright.
They lived out the fantasy essential to Wishart;
he might have been back in London saying and
thinking "Cannes." They had worked out their
code of intimate jokes for the season: they called
Bonnie's young friends *les fleurs et couronnes,*
and they made fun of French jargon with its
nervous emphasis on "moderne" and "dynamique." When Bonnie called Wishart *un homme
du vingtième siècle, moderne et dynamique,* they
were convulsed. Flor and Bob, a little apart, regarded them soberly, as if they were a pair of
chattering squirrels.

"Wishart is one of Mama's best friends," said
Flor, apologizing for this elderly foolishness.
"I've never liked him. I think he thinks they're
like Oberon and Titania, you know, all malice
and showing off. Wishart would love to have
wings and power and have people do as he says.
He's always seemed wormy to me. Have you
noticed that my mother pays for everything?"

In point of fact, Bob paid for everything now.
He expected to: it was as essential to his nature
as it was to Wishart's to giggle and sneer. To
amuse Bonnie, he had sneered about Bob.

"Wishart doesn't like the way I look because Wishart would like to look like nothing at all. The hell with him," he said placidly. He really was awfully pleased with himself: lying on her back on the sand, Flor shaded her eyes to see him properly. He was turned away. He seemed casual, indifferent, but she knew that he stayed on in Cannes because of her. His holiday was over, and his father, business and family-minded, was waiting for him in Paris. The discovery of Flor had disturbed him. Until now he had liked much younger girls with straight hair and mild, anxious eyes; girls who were photographed in the living room wearing printed silk and their mother's pearls. His ideal was the image of some minor Germanic princess, whose nickname might be Mousie, who seems to wear the same costume, the same hair, and the same air of patient supplication until a husband can be found. This picture, into which he had tried to fit so many women, now proved accommodating: the hair became red, the features hardened, the hands were thin and brown. She stared at him with less hopeless distress. At last the bland young woman became Flor, and he did not remember having held in his mind's eye any face but hers, just as he would never expect to look in the mirror one morning and see any face except his own.

These two people seemed to Wishart common objects, washed together by a tide of mutual mindlessness and simple desire. To oblige Bonnie, he pretended to see in Flor a courted darling, and Bob one of a chain of victims. "Bob is just a deep, creative boy looking for a girl with a tragic sense of life," he said to Bonnie, who laughed herself to tears, for, having tried to trap Bob into saying "stateside" and "drapes," and having failed, she needed new confirmation of his absurdity. The conversation of the pair, devoid of humor, was repeated by anyone close enough to hear. "Do you know what they're talking about *now?*" was a new opening for discussion, amazement, and, finally, helpless laughter.

"They're on birds today," Wishart said, with a deliberately solemn face.

"Birds?"

"Birds." They collapsed, heaving with laughter, as if in a fit. The *fleurs et couronnes,* out of sympathy, joined in.

"Do you know what bothered me most when I first came over here?" Wishart had heard Flor say. "We were in England then, and I didn't recognize a single tree or a single bird. They looked different, and the birds had different songs. A robin wasn't a robin any more. It was terrible. It frightened me more than anything. And they were so drab. Everything was brown and gray. There aren't any red-winged blackbirds, you know, nothing with a bright flash."

"Aren't there?" The urban boy tried to sound surprised. Wishart sympathized. The only quality he shared with Bob was ignorance of nature.

"Didn't you know? That's what's missing here, in everything. There's color enough, but you don't know how I miss it, the bright flash."

He saw the sun flash off a speedboat and everywhere he looked he saw color and light. The cars moving along the Croisette were color enough.

"Will you always live here now?" said Flor. "Will you never live at home again?"

"It depends on my father. I came over to learn, and I'm practically running the whole Paris end. It's something."

"Do you like business?"

"Do you mean do I wish I was an actor or something?" He gave her a resentful look and the shadow of their first possible difference fell over the exchange.

"My father never did anything much," she said. Her eyes were closed and she talked into the sun. The sun bleached her words. Any revelation was just talk. "Now they say he drinks quite a lot. But that's none of my business. He married a really dull thing, they say. He and Mama are Catholics so they don't believe in their own divorce. At least, Mama doesn't. I suppose he thinks he shouldn't be living with his second wife. If he still believes."

"How about you?"

"I'd believe anything I thought would do me or Mama any good."

This seemed to him insufficient. He expected

women to be religious. He gave any amount of money to nuns.

These dialogues, which Wishart heard from a distance while seeming to concentrate on his tan, and which he found so dull and discouraging that the pair seemed mentally deficient, were attempts to furnish the past. Flor was perplexed by their separate pasts. She saw Bob rather as Bonnie did, but with a natural loyalty that was almost as strong as a family tie. She believed she was objective, detached; then she discovered he had come down to Cannes from Paris with a Swedish girl, the student from whom he had inherited the cap. Knowing that "student" in Europe is a generous term, covering a boundless field of age as well as activity, she experienced the hopeless jealousy a woman feels for someone she believes inferior to herself. It was impossible for Bonnie's daughter to achieve this inferiority; she saw the man already lost. The girl and Bob had lived together, in his room, where Flor now went afternoons while Bonnie was having her rest. Flor's imagination constructed a spiteful picture of a girl being cute and Swedish and larking about in his pajamas. Secretly flattered, he said no, she was rather sickly and quiet. Her name was Eve. She was traveling on a bus. Cards arrived bearing the sticky imprint of her lips: a disgusting practice. Trembling with feigned indifference, Flor grabbed the hat and threw it out the window. It landed on the balcony of the room below.

Bob kept the cap, but he gave up his hotel and moved into Flor's. The new room was better. It was quiet, dark, and contained no memories. It was in the basement, with a window high on the wall. The walls were white. There was sand everywhere, in the cracked red tiles of the floor, in the chinks of the decaying armchair, caked to the rope soles of their shoes. It seemed to Flor that here the grit of sand and salt came into their lives, and their existence as a couple began. When the shutters were opened, late in the afternoon, they let in the peppery scent of geraniums and the view of a raked gravel path. There must have been a four-season mimosa nearby; the wind sent minute yellow pompons against the sill, and often a gust of sweetish perfume came in with the dying afternoon.

Flor had not mentioned the change to Bonnie, but, inevitably, Bonnie met her enemy at the desk, amiable and arrogant, collecting his key. "Has that boy been here all along?" she cried in despair. She insisted on seeing his room. She didn't know what she expected to find, but, as she told Wishart, she had a right to know. Bob invited her formally. She came with Flor one afternoon, both dressed in white, with skirts like lampshades, Bonnie on waves of "Femme." He saw for the first time that the two were alike and perhaps inseparable; they had a private casual way of speaking and laughed at the same things. It was like seeing a college friend in his own background, set against his parents, his sisters,

his mother's taste in books. He offered Bonnie
peanuts out of a tin, brandy in a toothbrush glass.
He saw everything about her except that she was
attractive, and here their difference of age was
in the way. Bob and Florence avoided sitting
on the lumpy bed, strewn with newspapers and
photographs. That was Bonnie's answer. They
knew she knew: Bonnie left in triumph, with an
air she soon had cause to change. Now that
Bonnie knew, the lovers spent more time together. They no longer slipped away during Bonnie's rest: they met when they chose and stayed
away as long as they liked. If they kept a pre-
tense of secrecy, it was because to Bob a façade
of decency was needed. He had not completely
lost sight of the beseeching princess into whose
outline Flor had disappeared.

When he and Flor were apart, he found reason
to doubt. She had told him the birds of Europe
were not like the birds at home, but what about
human beings? She never mentioned them. The
breath of life for him was contained in relations,
in his friendships, in which he did not distinguish
between the random and the intense. All his re-
lationships were of the same quality. She had
told him that this room was like a place she had
imagined. The only difference was that her imagined room was spangled, bright, perfectly silent, and full of mirrors. Years after this, he could
say to himself, Cannes, and evoke a season of his
life, with all the sounds, smells, light and dark

that the season had contained; but he never remembered accurately how it had started or what it had been like. Their intimacy came first, then love, and some unclouded moments. Like most lovers, he believed that the beginning was made up of these moments only, and he would remember Flor's silent, mirrored room, and believe it was their room at Cannes, and that he had lived in it too.

One afternoon at the beginning of July, they fell asleep in this room, the real room, and when Flor woke it was dark. She knew it had begun to rain by the quickening in the air. She got up quietly and opened the shutters. A car came into the hotel drive: a bar of light swept across the ceiling and walls. She thought that what she felt now came because of the passage of light: it was a concrete sensation of happiness, as if happiness could be felt, lifted, carried around. She had not experienced anything of the kind before. She was in a watery world of perceptions, where impulses, doubts, intentions, detached from their roots, rise to the surface and expand. The difference between Bob and herself was that he had no attachments to the past. This was what caused him to seem inferior in her mother's view of life. He had told them freely that his father was self-educated and that his mother's parents were illiterate. There were no family records more than a generation old. Florence had been taught to draw her support from continuity and the past.

Now she saw that the chain of fathers and daughters and mothers and sons had been powerless as a charm; in trouble, mistrusting her own capacity to think or move or enjoy living, she was alone. She saw that being positive of even a few things, that she was American, or pretty, or Christian, or Bonnie's girl, had not helped. Bob Harris didn't know his mother's maiden name, and his father's father had come out of a Polish ghetto, but he was not specifically less American than Florence, nor less proud. He was if anything more assertive and sure. She closed the shutters and came toward him, quietly, so that he would not wake and misinterpret her drawing near. Lacking an emotional country, it might be possible to consider another person one's home. She pressed her face against his unmoving arm, accepting everything imperfect, as one accepts a faulty but beloved country, or the language in which one's thoughts are formed. It was the most dangerous of ideas, this "only you can save me," but her need to think it was so overwhelming that she wondered if this was what men, in the past, had been trying to say when they had talked about love.

The rainstorm that afternoon was not enough. Everyone agreed more rain was needed. Rain was wanted to wash the sand, clean the sea, cool their tempers, rinse the hot roofs of the bathing cabins along the beach. When Wishart thought

"Cannes" now it was not light, dark, and blueness, but sand, and cigarette butts, and smears of oil. At night the heat and noise of traffic kept him awake. He lay patient and motionless with opened owl eyes. He and Bonnie compared headaches at breakfast: Bonnie's was like something swelling inside the brain, a cluster of balloons, while Wishart's was external, a leather band.

He could not understand what Bonnie was doing in this place; she had been so fastidious, rejecting a resort when it became too popular, seeming to him to have secret mysterious friends and places to go to. He still believed she would not be here, fighting through mobs of sweating strangers every time she wanted a slopped cup of coffee or a few inches of sand, if there had not been a reason — if she had not been expecting something real.

After a time he realized that Bonnie was not waiting for anything to happen, and that the air of expectancy that day had been false. If she had expected anything then, she must have believed it would come through him. She talked now of the futility of travel; she abandoned the Venus image of Flor, and said that Flor was cold and shallow and had broken her heart. There was no explanation for it, except that Flor was not fulfilling Bonnie's hopes and plans. Self-pity followed: she said that she, Bonnie, would spend the rest of her life like a bit of old paper on the

beach, cast up, beaten by waves, and so forth.
She didn't care what rubbish she talked and she
no longer tried to be gay. Once she said, "It's
no good, Wishart, she's never been a woman.
How can she feel what I feel? She's never even
had her periods. We've done everything, hor-
mones, God knows what all. I took her to Zurich.
She was so passive, she didn't seem to know it
was important. Sometimes I think she's dumb.
She has these men — I don't know how far she
goes. I think she's innocent. Yes, I really do. I
don't want to think too much. It's nauseating
when you start to think of your own daughter
that way. But she's cold. I know she's cold.
That's why we have no contact now. That's why
we have no contact any more. I've never stopped
being a woman. Thank God for it. If I haven't
married again it hasn't been because I haven't
men after me. Wishart! It's tragic for me to see
that girl. I'm fifty and I'm still a woman, and
she's twenty-four and a piece of ice."

He was lying beside her on the sand. He
pulled his straw hat over his face, perfectly appalled. It was a pure reaction, unplanned. If he
let his thoughts move without restraint into the
world of women, he discovered an area dimly
lighted and faintly disgusting, like a kitchen in
a slum. It was a world of migraines, miscarriage,
disorder, and tears.

Another day, complaining of how miserable
her life had been in Europe, she said, "I stopped

noticing when the seasons changed. Someone would say that the trees were in bud. I hadn't even noticed that the leaves were gone. I stopped noticing everything around me, I was so concentrated on Flor."

She talked to him about money, which was new. When he discovered she was poor, she dwindled to nothing, for then she had nothing to make her different or better than anyone else. She had always been careful over pennies, but he had believed it was the passionate stinginess of the rich. But she was no better than Wishart; she was dependent on bounty too. "I get no income at all, except from my brothers. And Stanley isn't required to support me, although he should, as I've had the burden of the child. And Flor's money is tied up in some crazy way until she's thirty. My father tied it up that way because of my divorce, he never trusted me again. Believe me, he paid for it. I never sent him as much as a postcard from that day until the day he died. Family, Wishart! God! Lovely people, but when it comes to m-o-n-e-y," she said, spelling it out. "Flor's allowance from Stanley was only until her majority and now he hardly sends her anything at all, he forgets, he isn't made to do anything. She'll have to wait now until he dies. They say the way he's living now there won't be anything left. Wishart, my brain clangs like a cash register when I think about it. I never used to worry at all, but now I can't stop."

"You thought she would be married by the time her allowance from Stanley stopped." No tone could make this less odious. He thought he had gone too far, and was blaming her for having started it, when she relieved him by being simply angry.

"Do you think it's easy? Marriage proposals don't grow on trees. I can't understand it. I had so many."

This was the beginning of the conversation they had had on the Croisette. It showed how worn their friendship had become. It was used down to the threads, they had no tolerance for each other any more, and nothing new to give. They were more intimate than they needed to be; he blamed her. *He* had tried to keep it bright. Once Bob had asked why Bonnie lived in Europe, and Wishart had replied, "Bonnie had Flor and then, worn out with childbearing, retired to a permanently sunny beach." This was a flattering version of Bonnie's divorce and flight from home. "Don't you listen," Bonnie said, immensely pleased. (She was pleased on another count: they were sitting on the outer edge of a café, and Bob was repeatedly jostled by the passing crowd. He had once said he liked people and didn't mind noise, and Bonnie saw to it that he had a basinful of both when it could be managed.) Wishart wanted their holiday to go on being as it had sounded when he said, in London, "I am going to Cannes to stay with a delightful American

friend." The American friend now questioned
Wishart about his plans. He perceived with horror that she was waiting for a suggestion from
him. He might have been flattered by Bonnie's
clinging to him, but in friendship he was like a
lover who can adore only in pursuit. In a few
days, he would be in Venice with Mrs. Sebastian
— blessed Mrs. Sebastian, authentically rich.
Snubbing Bonnie, he talked Venice to the *fleurs
et couronnes*. Rejected by Wishart, abandoned
by Flor, Bonnie took on a new expression; even
more than Wishart, she looked like the failed
comedian afflicted with dreams. He knew it, and
was pleased, as if in handing over a disease he
had reduced its malignant powers. Then, in time
to bump him off his high horse, Wishart received
a letter from Mrs. Sebastian putting him off until
August. There were no apologies and no explanations. She simply told him not to come. He
remembered then that she was cold and vulgar,
and that she drank too much, and that, although
she was a hefty piece, her nickname was Peewee
and she insisted on being given it; she was avari-
cious and had made Wishart pay her for a bottle
of DDT and a spray one summer when the mos-
quitoes were killing him. He remembered that
in American terms Bonnie was someone and Mrs.
Sebastian nothing at all. Bonnie became generous, decent, elegant, and essential to Wishart's
life. He turned to her as if he had been away;
but as far as she was concerned he *had* been

away, and he had lost ground. He regretted now
that he had failed to worship Venus-Flor, and
had not taken seriously Bonnie's earnest preoccu-
pation with Bob Harris, the one from Turkey,
and all the sots and lumpkins who had gone before. The dark glasses that seemed to condense
the long curve of the beach into a miniature image were averted now. Even a diminished peni-
tent Wishart could not find his own reflection.

For her part, Bonnie was finding her withering
Marchbanks tedious. His pursy prejudice no
longer seemed delicious humor. He made the
mistake of telling her a long name-studded story
of school politics and someone trying to get his
job. It established him in reality — a master
afraid for his grubby post — and reality was not
what Bonnie demanded. She had enough reality
on her hands: in the autumn that girl would be
twenty-five.

Wishart tried to get back on their old plane.
"Distract her," he said lazily. "Move on. Divert
her with culture. Inspect the cathedrals and museums. Take her to the Musée de l'Homme."

"You don't meet any men in museums," said
Bonnie, as if this were a sore point. "Anyway,
what's the good? She only comes to life for
slobs." After a moment she said quietly, "Don't
you see, that's not what I want for Flor. I don't
want her to marry just anybody. It may sound
funny to you, but I don't even want an American.
They've always let me down. My own brothers

. . . but I don't want to go into it again. I want a European, but not a Latin, and one who has lived in the States and has had the best of both. I want someone much older than Flor, because she needs that, and someone I can trust. That's what I want for my girl and that's what I meant when I said proposals don't grow on trees. Neither do men." But what did Wishart know about men? He was a woman-haunter, woman's best friend. She put on her sunglasses in order to hide her exasperation with him, because he was a man, but not the right person.

Her expression was perfectly blank. There was no doubt now, no other way of interpreting it. In spite of his recent indifference to her, she had not changed her mind. Wishart was being offered Flor.

He had never been foolish enough to dream of a useful marriage. He knew that his choice one season might damn him the next. He had thought occasionally of a charming but ignorant peasant child, whom he could train; he had the town boy's blurry vision of country people. Unfortunately, he had never met anyone of the kind. Certainly, his peasant bride, who was expected to combine with her exceptional beauty the fact that she wouldn't object to cleaning his shoes, was not Flor.

This was not the moment for false steps. He saw himself back in America with a lame-brained but perfect wife. Preposterous ideas made him

say in imagined conversations, The mother was
a charmer, I married the daughter.

He forgot the dangers, Bonnie as a mother-in-
law. A secret hope unfurled and spread. He got
up and in a blind determined way began to walk
across the beach. Not far away the lovers lay on
the sand, facing each other, half asleep. Flor's
arm was under her head, straight up. He saw
Bob's back, burned nearly black, and Flor's face.
They were so close that their breath must have
mingled. Flor's beauty decreased, became less
standard; he would not have called her a Venus
now. Their intimacy seemed to Wishart established; it contained an implicit allegiance, like a
family tie, with all the antagonism that might
suggest as well. They came together. Wishart
saw that Flor remained outside the kiss. Two
laurels with one root: where had he heard that?
Each was a missing part of the other's character,
and the whole, in the kiss, should have been un-
flawed.

Flor wondered what it was like for a man to
kiss her and remembered words from men she
had not loved. It was a narcissism so shameful
that she opened her eyes and saw Wishart. He
was the insect enemy met in an underground
tunnel, the small, scratching watcher, the bone-
less witness of an insect universe: a tiny, scuttling
universe that contained her mother, the pop-eyed
Corsican proprietor of this beach, the *fleurs et
couronnes,* her mother's procession of very best

most intimate friends — before Wishart, a bestial
countess to whom Flor, as a girl, had been in-
structed to be nice. In a spasm of terror that Bob
mistook for abandonment, she clung to him; he
was outside this universe and from a better place.

Wishart returned to Bonnie and sank down
beside her on the sand, adjusting his bony legs
as if they were collapsible umbrellas. If he continued in error it was Bonnie's fault, for she went
on again about men, the right man, and Flor.
The wind dropped: Cannes settled into the stag-
nant afternoon. The *fleurs et couronnes* were
down from their naps and chattering like budg-
erigars. Bonnie had been polishing her sunglasses on the edge of a towel. She stopped,
holding them, staring. "Last night I dreamed
my daughter was a mermaid," she said. "What
does it mean? Wishart, you know all about those
things. What does it mean?"

"*Ravissant*," said one of her court. "I see the
blue sea, and the grottoes, everything coral and
blue. Coral green and coral blue."

"There is no such thing as coral blue," said
Wishart mechanically.

"And Florence, *la belle Florence*, floating and
drifting, the bright hair spread like . . ."

"She sang and she floated, she floated and
sang," took up a minor figure who resembled a
guppy. At a look from Bonnie he gave a great
gasp and shut up.

"It was nothing like that at all," said Bonnie

snappily. "It was an ugly fish tail, like a carp's. It was just like a carp's and the whole thing was a great handicap. The girl simply couldn't walk. She lay there on the ground and couldn't do a thing. Everybody stared at us. It was a perfectly hopeless dream and I woke up in a state of *great distress*."

Wishart had been so disturbed by the kiss that moved into blankness. He could not form a coherent thought. What interested him, finally, was the confirmation for Flor as a *poseuse*. How conceited she had been, lying there, exploring her own sensations as idly as tourists turning sand from one hand into the other. He recalled the expression in her eyes — shrewd, ratty eyes, he thought, not the eyes of a goddess — and he knew that she feared and loathed him and might catch him out. "It won't do," he said to Bonnie, or "It wouldn't do, a marriage with Flor." He heard the words, "she has a crack across the brain," but was never certain if he had said them aloud. Bonnie turned her pink, shadowed face to him in purest amazement. She noticed that Wishart's eyes were so perturbed and desperate that they were almost beyond emotion, without feeling, like those of a bird. Then she looked up to the sky, where the plane was endlessly and silently writing the name of a drink. She said, "I wish he would write something for us, something useful."

His mistake had been greater than the gaffe about Flor. Everything trembled and changed;

even the color of the sky seemed extraordinary. Wishart was fixed and paralyzed in this new landscape, wondering if he was doing or saying anything strange, unable to see or stop himself. It was years since he had been the victim of such a fright. He had believed that Bonnie accepted him at his value. He had believed that the exact miniature he saw in her sunglasses was the Wishart she accepted, the gentleman he had glimpsed in the store window that first day. He had thought that the inflection of a voice, the use of some words, established them as a kind. But Bonnie had never believed in it. She had never considered him anything but jumped-up. He remembered now that she had never let him know her family back home, had never suggested he meet her brothers.

When Bonnie dared look again Wishart was picking his way into the sea. He was wearing his hat. He did not mind looking foolish and believed eccentricity added to his stature. After standing for a time, knee-deep, looking with the expression of a brooding camel first at the horizon and then back to shore, he began to pick his way out again. The water was too dirty for swimming, even if the other bathers had left him room. "Large colored balls were being flung over my head and some things against it," he composed, describing for future audiences the summer at Cannes. "The shrieking children of butchers were being taught to swim."

Farther along the beach Bob Harris carried

two bottles of beer, crowned with inverted glasses, down to Flor. Bonnie watched without emotion. Their figures were motionless, to be printed against her memory, arrested in heat and the insupportable noise.

Everyone around Bonnie was asleep. The sirocco, unsteady, pulled her parasol about on the sand. Sitting, knees bent, she clasped her own white feet. There was not a blemish on them; the toes were straight, the heels rosy. She had tended her feet like twin infants, setting an example for Flor. Once, exasperated by Flor's neglect, she had gone down on her knees and taken Flor's feet on her lap and shown her how it ought to be done. She had creamed and manicured and pumiced while Flor, listless, surreptitiously trying to get on with a book, said, "Oh, Mama, I can do it." "But you won't, honey. You simply don't take care of yourself unless I'm there." She had polished and tended her little idol, and for whom? For a Turk not sixty-three inches high. For Bob Harris in tartan trunks. It was no use; the minutes and hours had passed too quickly. She was perplexed by the truth that had bothered her all her life, that there was no distance between time and events. Everything raced to a point beyond her reach and sight. Everyone slid out of her grasp: her husband, her daughter, her friends. She let herself fall back. Her field of vision closed in and from the left came the first, swimming molecules of pain.

Wishart, coming out of the teeming sea, making a detour to avoid being caught up and battered in a volley-ball game, came up to Bonnie unobserved. Patting his yellowed skin with a towel he watched the evolution of his friend's attack. Her face was half in sun. She twisted to find the shadow of the rolling parasol. Bitter, withdrawn, he was already pulling about himself the rags of imaginary Wishart: the squire father, Mrs. Sebastian rolling in money above the Grand Canal. Bonnie believed she was really dying this time, and wondered if Flor could see.

Flor said, "I think Mama has one of her headaches."

"You two watch each other, don't you?" He had asked why she said "Mama" and had been told it was a habit of the Fairlies, her mother's family. She said it as she might have explained, "Everybody in our family has used the same toothbrush since nineteen twelve."

A haze had gone over the sky. She finished her beer, spread her striped beach towel a little away from him, and lay still. He had told her that his father had telephoned from Paris, and that this time it was an order. He was leaving soon, perhaps the next day. This was July. The summer, a fruit already emptied by wasps, still hung to its tree. He was leaving. When he had gone, she would hear the question, the ghost voice that speaks to every traveler, Why did you come to this place? Until now, she had known: she was somewhere or other with her mother because her mother could not settle down, because every rented flat and villa was a horrible parody of home, or the home she ought to have given Flor. When he had gone, she would know without illusion that she was in Cannes in a rotting season, the rot was reality, and there was no hope in the mirrored room.

"Are you coming to Paris later on?" His father was waiting; he spoke with a sense of urgency, like someone trying to ring off, holding the receiver, eyes wandering around the room.

"I don't know. I don't know where we'll go from here, or how long Mama will stay. She and Wishart always finish with a fight, and Mama loses her head, and we go rushing off. All our relations at home think we have such a glamorous life. Did you ever go out in the morning and find a spider's web spangled with dew?" she said suddenly. "You'll never find that here. It's either too hot and dry, or it rains so much the spider drowns. At my grandmother's place, you know, summers, I used to ride, oh, early, early in the morning, with my cousins. All my cousins were boys." Her voice was lost as she turned her head away.

"Flor, why don't you go home?"

"I can't leave my mother, and she won't go. Maybe I don't dare. She used to need me. Maybe now I need her. What would I do at home? My grandmother is dead. I haven't got a home. I know I sound as if I feel sorry for myself, but I haven't got anything."

"You've got your mother," he said. "There's me."

Now it was here, the circumstance that Bonnie had loathed and desired. He moved closer and spoke with his lips to her ear, playing with her hair, as if they were alone on the beach or in his room. He remembered the basement room as if they would never be in it again. He remembered her long hair, the wrinkled sheets, the blanket thrown back because of the heat. It was the prophetic instant, the compression of feeling that occurs in childhood and in dreams. Wishart passed by: his shadow fell over their feet. They were obliged to look up and see his onion skin and pickled eyes. They were polite. No one could have said that they had agreed to change the movement of four lives, and had diverted the hopes, desires, and ambitions of Bonnie and of Bob's father, guides whose direction had suddenly failed.

Wishart went back to his hotel. It was the hour when people who lived in *pensions* began to straggle up from the sea. Whole families got in Wishart's way. They were badly sunburned, smelled of Ambre Solaire and Skol, and looked as if they couldn't stand one another's company another day. Wishart bathed and changed. He walked to the post office and then to the station to see about a bus. He was drily forgiving when people stepped on his feet, but looked like someone who will never accept an apology again. He sent a telegram to an American couple he knew who had a house near Grasse. He had planned to skip them this year; the husband disliked him. (The only kind of husband Wishart felt easy with was the mere morsel, the half-digested scrap.) But he could not stay on with Bonnie now, and Mrs. Sebastian had put him off. He put his full horror of Cannes into a heartrending message that began "Very depressed" but he did not sign a funny name for fear of making the husband cross. He signed his own name and pocketed the change and went off to the station. This time he and Bonnie were parting without a quarrel.

That night there was a full moon. Bonnie woke up suddenly as if she had become conscious of a thief in the room; but it was only Flor, wearing the torn bathrobe she had owned since she was fourteen, and that Bonnie never managed to throw away. She was holding a glass of water in her hand, and looking down at her sleeping mother. "Flor, is anything wrong?"

"I was thirsty." She put the glass on the night table and sank down beside her mother on the floor.

"That Wishart," said Bonnie, now fully awake, and beginning to stroke Flor's hair. "He really takes himself for something."

"What is he taking himself for?"

Bonnie stroked her daughter's hair, thinking, My mermaid, my prize. The carp had vanished from the dream, leaving an iridescent Flor. No one was good enough for Florence. That was the meaning of the dream. "Your hair is so stiff, honey, it's full of salt. I wish you'd wear a bathing cap. Flor, have you got a fever or something?" She wants to tell me something, Bonnie thought. Let it be anything except about that boy. Let it be anything but that.

At dawn, Wishart, who had been awake most of the night, buckled his suitcase. No porter was around at that hour. He walked to the station in streets where there was still no suggestion of the terrible day. The southern scent, the thin distillation of lemons and geraniums, descended from the hills. Then heat began to tremble; Vespas raced along the port; the white-legged grub tourists came down from the early train. Wishart thought of his new hostess, academic, a husk; she chose the country behind Grasse because of the shades of Gide and Saint-Ex; ghosts who would keep away from her if they knew what was good for them. He climbed into the bus and sat down among workingmen who had jobs in Grasse, and the sea dropped behind him as he was borne away.

In the rocking bus his head dropped. He knew that he was in a bus and traveling to Grasse, but he saw Glad, aged twelve, going off at dawn with her lunch wrapped in an apron. What about the dirty, snotty baby boy who hung on her dress, whose fingers she had to pry loose one at a time only to have the hand clamp shut again, tighter than before? Could this be Wishart, clinging, whining, crying, "Stay with me"? But Wishart was awake and not to be trapped. He took good care not to dream, and when the bus drew in at Grasse, under the trees, and he saw his new straw-thin hostess (chignon, espadrilles, peasant garden hat) he did not look like a failed actor assailed with nightmares, but a smooth and pleasant schoolmaster whose sleep is so deep that he never dreams at all.

IV
IV
IV
IV
IV
IV

FOR ALL THE reaction he was getting he might as well have been alone. When he spoke, no one replied. So far, no one had said, "How thoughtful of you, George," although it was he who had chosen the table in the bar, where they could be quiet and alone, instead of the crowded dining room. Dinner was over. The waiter leaned on the bar, adding up the check, counting, as though he couldn't believe the total, the bottles of wine and rounds of brandy. The bartender read a spread-out newspaper. George's Aunt Bonnie was pushing herself into a bolero of monkey fur; she had irritably waved away his offers of help. There was a third person at the table, his aunt's son-in-law, Bob Harris. Harris couldn't see Aunt Bonnie's struggles: his elbows were on the table, his face behind his hands. George observed, as part of a still-suspended opinion, that Harris wore two rings, one that was modern and gold and matched his cuff links, and a small onyx, squeezed onto the little finger of his left hand. It looked like a woman's ring. Perhaps it had belonged to Harris's wife.

"It's f-funny," George began again. He was trying to say that there was a funny light over the Louvre, as if beams of warm, theatrical color were being played from somewhere behind — from the rue de Rivoli, for instance. The windows of the Left Bank bar where they had dined gave on this sight, which was nothing more than the last blaze of day. George had been looking for themes of conversation and he was now trying this. Nobody cared.

"This dinner is on me," said George, despairingly, to Harris's still hidden face.

At that moment the waiter sprang to help George's aunt. Twisting, craning, waving her thin arms, she wrestled with the bolero. Now it was inside out. The waiter removed it, shook it, guided Aunt Bonnie's groping hands. "*Merci*. Now what did you want, Georgie dear?" But by now it was night. Nothing remained except a vanishing saffron cloud.

Harris sat back with his hands on the table, smiling faintly, so full of himself, so smooth, that George wondered if the grieving movement had not been something dreamt. Often in his childhood he had been assured that a dramatic moment clearly seen and heard had never taken place. Harris nodded at the waiter: "There's your bill," and the waiter bent over George with the check folded on a plate, and a pencil so that he could sign. Harris seemed to enjoy using English expressions such as "bill." The dark clothes he wore gave him a grave, foreign air, and he appeared older than his age, which was twenty-six or seven. He had a dark, soft face, and might have been a Greek or a Persian educated in England, if one took the sum of his face, his manner, his rings, and his clothes. In a letter home Aunt Bonnie had said that her son-in-law looked like a suburban gangster. To George, Harris was neither foreign nor gangster, nor suburban, nor entirely respectable. He was familiar in a distinctly American way, but he was not the kind of American George had been brought up to know well. In strange Paris, he was as complete in familiarity as someone from George's own world might have been, although different in quality — urban, sharp. He watched George's troubles without offering to help. George was grateful for that. The spurt of assurance that made him demand a table in the bar, and insist dinner be served there, had damped out. His stammer was back. He was not sure of his French. For a minute he had been decisive, representing the male element in Aunt Bonnie's family. The minute ended, he was George again, with everything being George implied, at least to himself. He had to explain to this waiter that he was not staying at the hotel. That he therefore couldn't sign the bill. That he wanted to pay with a traveler's check and be given his change in francs. He brought it off as if he had been entertaining in foreign restaurants all his life, and Harris helped by keeping out; not so Aunt Bonnie, who screamed, "We're not really going to let this little boy pay for that meal?"

Poor Aunt Bonnie had put herself in a costume so grotesque that anything she had to say was dimmed. Her clothes must have come out of a trunk: they smelled of camphor and the dark — the fur, the sagging dress of black chiffon, the ropes of amber and jet, her pointed satin shoes, the purse with its chain handle and amber clasp. Her hair seemed to George dyed. He could not remember if his aunt had been wearing this head of hair when he had seen her two years before. The space between his having been seventeen, and at home, and being nineteen, and abroad, could not be measured by any system known to him; not even by the changes in people he knew.

Aunt Bonnie dabbed at her lipstick with an embroidered handkerchief. "You're a real Fairlie, George," she said. "That was a nice meal." In spite of her grief she had eaten melon, chicken, salad, cheese, and ice cream. She had refused everyone's cigarettes, sending out for a brand of her own, and had complained about the wines. Sometimes she let her head hang as if her neck had snapped, then she would suddenly look, and speak, and glance at George with his father's blue eyes. As for Harris, he simply behaved as if he were alone.

George didn't notice when Harris left the table, so easily did he slide away, until Aunt Bonnie put her powdered face next to his and said, "He's gone to take care of the bill and get your check back for you. Now, don't say a word when he comes back. Don't thank him. He likes doing these things. George, I don't know what I would do now without Bob. He was so awfully nice to her. He was just so nice to her all the time. Florence could be trying. Oh, yes, she was an angel itself, but she could be trying too. I know you don't think so, you only saw the good side, she loved you so. But that boy was married to her, he had to live with her, just as I had to live with her, and he was just nice to her all the time."

"*You* didn't have to live with her," George said. It was the kind of statement that went out of his mouth before it was through his mind; it was just an intention, not even a thought. He looked at his aunt in perfect dismay, as though she had said something strange; but Aunt Bonnie said amiably, "Why darling, Flor and I were so close, you know. She'd have been miserable without me, always worried. And I'd have worried about her. It wouldn't have been fair to Bob, leaving him with this worried girl on his hands. I mattered terribly in their marriage, dear. I used to think of myself as a kind of lightning rod."

"Nobody, *nobody* ever gets the better of Bonnie," George's father had once said. "She's sweet, she's helpless, she's had some stinking deals. But nobody ever gets the better of her. This Harris had better be tough." They hadn't known much about Harris then, except that Aunt Bonnie didn't like him. Florence met him on a beach or in a hotel and married him straightaway. She didn't care what people said and she wiped out with one gesture all the care and love and planning — but those were Aunt Bonnie's words. She had been mournful, poor Aunt Bonnie, with her only girl gone to waste; she never saw it as anything less.

Aunt Bonnie seemed to have forgotten her old objections now. "Flor loved him," she crooned. "Yes, she did. He was so nice to her, you see. Flor had a lot of love in her." Abruptly she changed her tone, became matter-of-fact: "Bob went out to see her today, without me. They don't let us see her together, *I* don't know why. He said she was as loving as could be. She didn't know his name or anything but she put her head on his shoulder and stroked his face and she made him eat little pieces of bread from her tray. You see, even now she's full of love." Then Aunt Bonnie drew back and cried, "I was just saying, I wish Georgie knew someone in Paris more fun than us. He's not having a good time, he says."

Harris had returned and stood by the table

George's reflexes were slow. The falsehood, the outrage, the impertinence of his aunt made him stammer in his mind. As if he would have complained; as if, to these stricken people dressed in mock mourning, he could have complained. He wished Harris would look at him so that he could signal it wasn't true.

"We could do something later," Harris said in a neutral voice. "Whatever he wants."

"Do," said Aunt Bonnie warmly. "Oh, do. Florence would want you to be having fun."

The stupidity of the remark did not make it less cruel. George put himself in Harris's place and felt sick. He took refuge in contemplating the walls of the bar, which were papered with maps of Paris. He tried to find the names of streets. When he came back to his aunt and Harris again he saw they were looking away from each other. They seemed bewildered. Each was the witness of the other's suffering and that must have been terrible to bear. Harris probably wasn't taking in half the foolish things she said. He looked like a man who had come into a known station only to find all the trains going to the wrong places or leaving at impossible times: endlessly patient, he was waiting for the schedules to be rearranged.

"I'll g-go pay the check," said George, for something to say.

"You already have," said Harris. "Don't you remember?"

"Georgie thought *you'd* gone to pay it when you sneaked away like that," Aunt Bonnie said. She got up and scraped together her scarf, purse, fan, and gloves and tottered toward the door. She walked like a crone; she seemed to have made up her mind to be old and tactless, and dress like the Mad Woman of Chaillot. "I want to walk home," she said from the door. "I want to walk all the way home. You boys can come back after and pick up the car. I want to walk the way Florence used to walk. Florence loved the Paris night."

The night Florence had loved met them with the noise of traffic. The Seine was oily and still. This was the end of summer and the city seemed depleted by the season just endured; the heart of the city was emptied by the number of strangers on the streets, the motion of cars and boats, the prying searchlights on the monuments, the pressure of hands, feet, cameras, eyes. George had instantly felt it when he arrived from London that afternoon. If London could be described as too thick, Paris was too thin. He was glad this ruined holiday was over. He was glad he would soon be going home and no longer obliged to think and compare and consider the very quality of the air he took in.

"Lovely!" cried Aunt Bonnie, turning her sharp nose up to the sky. She gave an arm to each of the men. George took the fan and gloves, Harris the scarf and purse. He seemed at ease,

but George felt as if he were carrying twenty
fans and eighty pairs of gloves. He thought of
the White Rabbit, whom he suspected he resembled. His aunt pattered across the street, George
stumbled, and only Harris managed a normal
walk. They stopped on the Seine side of the
Quai Voltaire and the men waited for orders.
The whole thing had got into Aunt Bonnie's
hands. "I want to go along the quais," she de-
creed, "and over to the right bank on the Pont
de l'Alma, and up the Avenue Montaigne, and
home. It's a long walk, but Georgie should see
Paris."

George waited for Harris to object; it seemed
to him an insanely long walk. But Harris nodded
his head and they went on again — the oddest
trio you could imagine, George thought, unused
to oddity. Nothing had prepared him for this
situation, in which he kept trying to find his feet.
"George is so lucky," his mother had once said.
"He's had all the good disadvantages." His train-
ing was planned for the social rather than the
human collapse. His shed youth now seemed a
piling-up of hallucinations, things heard and seen
that were untrue or of no use to him. He was a
tall person with large hands and feet, light blue
eyes, and pale brows, lashes, and hair. His expression was earnest and kind. He had the voice
and manner of his father's family and he wore
the family face; it was an undistinguished sweet-
tempered face that usually triumphed over ad-

mixtures. One of Aunt Bonnie's sisters, George's Aunt Louise, had married a man named Reed; the Reed boys — there were four — were so violently Fairlie, flax-blond, ham-handed, that the Reed parent (bony, brown) might have had no chromosomes at all and Aunt Louise's doubled in number to compensate. George would have considered this a natural law: their features were a concrete heritage, like the rings, brooches, and cups that passed without visible friction from one unit to the next. There was a family personality — decent, generous, conceited — and they carried their upbringing like a grain of sand on the heart.

They walked slowly now, all three in step, in and out of lamplight and the shadows of leaves. "I think you're a brave boy, Georgie, coming to Europe alone," his aunt said. "All alone in England! Flor never went anywhere without me. Do you feel brave?"

"Actually, it was pretty lonesome," George said. He hoped that nothing in his tone admitted how lonesome it had been; there would have been something degrading in sharing the truth that his holiday had failed. "I wouldn't do it like this again. I liked some things in England. I liked Scotland more. But when I got here this afternoon I was so lonesome I didn't know what to do. I went around to your place but nobody came to the door. I kept on phoning . . ." Did this sound like self-pity? He had been around to see them: nobody home. That was casual enough. Back in his hotel, he had telephoned. He heard the ringing for the tenth time and then Bob's voice, civil, surprised, "*George?* Your aunt isn't here just now, George, but I'm expecting her. Florence isn't too well. We've had to take her to a place . . . a sort of rest place. Your aunt'll tell you. Didn't you get the telegram? I guess you didn't. We thought maybe you shouldn't come." His voice was soft, for a man, full of the sounds and rhythms that meant New York. This came over to George with wild familiarity. Across Paris, the voice conveyed the existence of seasons, mornings, afternoons. The voice was not in the least like his own; the good disadvantages had been provided in a sense so that he would never sound like Bob. "Where are you, George?" said the voice. "Have you got a pencil or something?" He gave the name of a restaurant in a hotel not far from George's own and said he would be along shortly with George's aunt. Everything pertaining to danger and grief flowed and settled around that talk, leaving George free to stroll by the Seine with his aunt, holding her fan and her gloves.

"Of course Georgie's lonely," said his aunt. "No good being in Paris unless you're in love, eh?" and she tweaked her son-in-law's dark sleeve.

She didn't know what she was saying any more. That was the only explanation. She had gone crazy with shock. George heard Bob say, "Don't worry," as though he hadn't listened to her in years but had an answer for her comments and complaints.

"You need to be in love," his aunt said, so wickedly, her hand jumping now on George's arm, that he knew it was intended for him. That meant his mother had written about Barbara Sim. It had gone on for years: for four summers. When he was eighteen it was over. It was over for him, that is; not for her. Gracelessly, she persisted in loving. One day the thought of Barbara was shadowed by the memory of Flor. Flor had nothing to do with Barbara, didn't know she existed. But George remembered what it had been like to be with Flor just as, through a hole in time, one goes back to a lake, a room in a city, or the south. It was probably because of the bead. He had grasped it out of habit and it lay in his hand. It was the cheap glass bead from the necklace his cousin had broken when she was fourteen. He saw her hands flying outward and the burst of glass like water flying. When he thought about his cousin that was what he saw: a thin sunburned girl pulling on a string of beads and making the string break. She was frightening to him then; he was only seven. She had what Aunt Bonnie called "cold bad tempers." No matter what had happened since (the scene of the "little pieces of bread" was a swampy horror on which his mind refused to alight) she was fixed then and now and for all his life: a wild girl breaking a necklace, the circle of life closing in at fourteen, the family, the mother, the husband to come.

George kept the bead as if he had already known, when he was seven, that he was a sort of coward, and needed tokens in his hand. Soon after he had written the final, classic letter to Barbara he lost the bead. He put his hand in his pocket and the bead was gone. What remained was his habit of clutching air. He was still a coward, and too polite.

George's parents had followed the romance with Barbara first with indulgence and then with alarm. Now they could smile: George was not going to ruin his life with that girl. He thought they should have known better; he would never ruin his life over anybody. He had been accustomed for so many years to Barbara, to writing or telling her nearly everything, that it was to Barbara, now, he confided that his parents had got it wrong, and his mother had betrayed him to Aunt Bonnie. Then his eyes met the eyes of a girl coming toward them. The girl emerged in the most poetic way imaginable, out of the Paris night. That was the way he wanted something to happen; that was the thing he was ready for now. The girl held his gaze until she was level with the three of them and then she glanced away. She was fair, with high cheekbones, and wore a tight gray skirt and a suede coat.

"Nursemaid," said Aunt Bonnie into the night.

"Millions of them come from Scandinavia every year. Warm little loves. They are supposed to be learning French."

She must always have been like that, a small bony cat waiting to jump. He decided to remember, in case it should ever be of any importance, that he had seen this girl on the Quai Anatole France. Aunt Bonnie moved with quick hopping steps, like a bird. She seemed to be enjoying the walk. She had always been the ailing one, but she had survived, and here she was, bobbing along, wound like a vine on the arms of two men, enjoying the night. The quai was quiet with the silence of a country road. Then they reached the Pont de la Concorde and the silence came to an end. A river of cars faster than the Seine ran past them and he saw at the other end of the bridge the lights of the Place de la Concorde strung unevenly, haunting and moving as the memory of lights across a lake, and the obelisk like a great lighted mast. "It's wonderful," he said dutifully. "But it sort of isn't a city." The answer, which should have come from Harris, was Aunt Bonnie's. She said as if it were wrenched from the heart: "New York is the only city." Her voice then resumed an artificial quaver; she had forgotten she was supposed to be an old lady. Now she remembered again. "If there was one thing my Florence hated, it was the way they light up all the monuments and things for the tourists. She said it made Paris loom like an old prostitute. She never would

look. As a matter of fact, she hardly ever went
out at night."

Half an hour earlier she had said that Florence
loved the Paris night; but contradiction seemed
to be typical of his aunt. She had told George
that Harris was generous and kind, whereas in
letters home she complained he was tight and
thoughtless and had never given them — the
women — a car. George couldn't very well ask,
Are you stingy? even though Harris was there
and able to defend himself — unlike Flor, who
was past choosing. Now he became physically
aware of the absence of Flor. He wondered
where she was: in a sort of convalescent place,
he supposed, hospital disguised as hotel where
there was a significance, unknown to him, in the
sound of a tap turned on or the color blue. Wondering where she was *really* he suspected she
was in no special place. She was not anywhere.
It would be nice to believe she was happier,
calmer, more loving than ever, but he thought
she was not anywhere.

The minute George went too far in his specu-
lations he lost hold of the real situation. He could
see three people walking, stopping for traffic,
moving on; he could hear their voices, but he
could not understand any of the things they said.
That was normal; this had been a terrible day:
there had been the journey from London, the
transition, the idea of coming to Paris ("all un-
suspecting . . ." as he kept telling himself), and
then the telephone ringing in an unseen room,

and Bob's voice saying, "Your aunt isn't here."
His aunt's hand lay light now on George's arm,
but her left hand clutched her son-in-law's
sleeve, and he stroked her arm, muttering in his
absent-minded way, "Don't worry" — the steady
answer for keeping his female family quiet.
They seemed to be joined for life, and, before
thinking and deciding not to say it, George said,
"God, I feel sorry for you, Bob," which would
go down as another of the famous George remarks.

"You don't have to be," said Bob after a moment. "I knew when I met Flor there weren't
two like her. She was never too much of anything. She had just enough. Just enough looks,
just enough brains, just enough of what Bonnie
here would call breeding." Aunt Bonnie began
to flash in all directions and even George thought
his cousin and the whole family with her were
being undervalued. He wanted to say, Flor isn't
queer from *our* side; as though Bob had anything
to do with that! Well, Bob was being cool and
objective now, but he hadn't behaved that way
two years ago, on his honeymoon, because
George had met him and he had seen and he
remembered. This was probably a way of not
hurting himself more than he could help, this
distant "just enough," but George knew. Pres-
ently he realized that what Bob had said bore
no relation to George's remark. It was simply a
statement given into the night.

"What Flor had more of I think was a kind of purity," said Aunt Bonnie sadly. "You know, Georgie, when she was little, she never asked me one embarrassing question, you know what I mean, and as she wasn't the kind of girl other little girls would tell anything nasty to, well, she was spared all the shocks. She was fortunate," said Aunt Bonnie, "she grew up without any shocks. I don't suppose you did," she said, plucking at George's sleeve. Bob was abandoned. Georgie was her boy now. He saw that he was being made to change roles with Flor, and that George, who had grown up safely at home, over-loved and overspoiled, was to be fitted out as his cousin — parents divorced, brought up just any-where, breaking years of silence to send her fa-ther letters of abuse, quarreling in public with her mother and having public remorse. They were creating an unmarred Florence, and through her a spotless Bonnie; no one was to be blamed for anything. "I wouldn't have wanted a son," Aunt Bonnie said. "Your daughter's your daughter all your life. You know what *your* mother wrote me last spring, Georgie? She wrote, 'It's hard to understand it but he'll soon be fin-ished with us.' And you were what, eighteen? Why, Flor at eighteen was like a little baby. She was never finished with me."

George thought, She is now.

Of course, he had said it. This time his reac-tion over the blunder was against the others. He

was sick of his mistakes. He was sick of Aunt
Bonnie and sick of Flor. If he had still owned
the bead he would have got rid of it now. He
would have reached out his hand and left it on
the low wall beside the quai. He was sick of his
aunt and he didn't like her. She was silly and
mischievous and he didn't like her at all. It was
all wrong, because she was in trouble now and
he was part of the family; but there was no jus-
tice in liking and not liking people. He loved his
parents, but here he was in Paris, without them.
What his mother had said in the letter was true:
he would soon be finished. He had loved Barbara but when he went to college he shook her
off — couldn't shake her off fast enough. Hate
might be easier than love, but he had never hated
anybody and as far as he knew only one person
had ever hated him, and that was Flor. He had
seen it when he was seven and she was fourteen,
and it was all the way she had turned her head
and let him see her eyes. Perhaps she hated him
because he was smug and fat and his parents
adored him; or perhaps he was reading too much
into that memory and she had behaved the way
an impatient girl of fourteen might be with any
small cousin who was a pest and a brat. His vanity was crucially engaged, for it was hard to swal-
low, even now, that, twelve years ago, Flor had
hated Georgie Fairlie, whom everyone was supposed to love.

Aunt Bonnie brought him down to earth. It
was one of her switches from nonsense to truth.

Her voice would alter at such times and would become hard, practical, quite funny, a little bit hoarse, as if she were the sort of woman who might call a waitress "dear." She had levels of voice for her levels of truth. Now she dropped into reality and her voice hardened and fell. She seemed closer to George, and he had the feeling of walking with someone he knew, not watching three unknown people pacing into the foreign night. "You know, Georgie," said his aunt, turning to him, laughing like a girl, "one time Flor got herself mixed up with a fellow from Egypt. He said he had been something or other once, or his father had been. I never knew a girl like her for getting in with people who had been something but weren't now. He said that when all the troubles in the Middle East were over he would take Flor to Egypt and he would show her the nightclub where King Farouk used to go and where he used to go himself when he was a young bachelor. I may say he wasn't a bachelor any more but that was another of Flor's specialities, she always met them too late in more ways than one. Flor said what happens in this nightclub, and he said, oh you see such lovely girls. In this club you see toutes les Miss de l'Europe. Now, to Flor une Miss was a governess, but it turned out he didn't mean that. He meant Miss Oslo, Miss Vichy Water, Miss Baden-Baden. That was what he wanted to show my Flor, Georgie, toutes les Miss de l'Europe."

George laughed and then thought of Harris

and stopped. They seemed to have been walking all night, halting, waiting for green lights, walking again. Harris was their guide. George was ashamed to look at him after Aunt Bonnie's story, but when they were on the Pont de l'Alma, obeying Aunt Bonnie's order to stop and see how beautiful the lighted bridges were, Bob leaned forward a little so that George could see his profile without seeming to stare. He was not the sleek, eager young man he remembered from the wedding trip, two years before, but someone soft and patient with the empty profile of the blind. He heard Harris say, "I used to wish we could be simple, but she couldn't be simple with the life she's had." The Seine was moving faster; the reflection of bridges cracked and shook. Bonnie took no notice of this plain provocation on the part of Bob and George guessed she hadn't heard: she had, though, for, choosing her moment, she said in an invalid's voice, "I can't ever tell you how sweet Florence was, George. Sweet and simple. And she was a high-spirited attractive girl. She could have had any one of a dozen tremendous men. A man tried to drown himself over Flor when she was only sixteen. Up there . . ." and she raised George's arm with her own to point back the way they had come.

"Don't worry," said Flor's husband soothingly. "Don't worry about a thing." He got his little group moving again and they went on. They were crossing into a different part of the city and

Bob seemed rekindled with every step. This was
his country: shops, nightclubs, well-dressed girls.
He was emerging from the role that had been
forced on him; he left off being soft and patient,
neutral and blind. It had been their fault. They
had excluded him. After all, he was the husband.
George wanted to tell him, You know about Aunt
Bonnie; it's only because I'm family, I use family
words, I'm home. How could he explain that
when she had said, "You're a real Fairlie," it left
out Bob but took in Flor? Or what a comfort it
was now, on the Pont de l'Alma, when everything said was wrong or hurting, to know that
his features were armor and his behavior a
shield? He tried to remember Flor, so as to place
her in the family ranks; but her face kept avoid-
ing him, like the girl seen that night and already
lost. He supposed Flor was pretty; people said
so. He forgot that he had once said so too. Now
he thought, She had too much McCarthy in her,
her eyes were too green. Then the face turned
abruptly toward him and he could see her eyes,
her mouth, and the part of her hair. He remembered Flor being very pretty, and proud, and he
remembered her lifting her thick hair with her
hands and looking around — as George's mother
said, "knowing it." She couldn't help knowing:
she probably looked in mirrors. "Flor was all
Fairlie," Aunt Bonnie had said during dinner,
as though Florence were dead. If she went on
like that, in no time she would believe, and make

George agree, that her daughter's hair was blond, her eyes blue. Flor was not anywhere now, so perhaps it didn't matter. Perhaps it was courtesy to accept the mother's mistakes. But he was stubborn and he knew that his isolated memories of Flor were right and Aunt Bonnie's fantasies wrong. He knew that Flor had red hair and a cold bad temper and perhaps didn't, or couldn't, care much for anything outside the span of the necklace. Bob, encased in silence and false calm, knew even more; but it was better not to explore that country. "I thought about Flor," said George, meaning that he had thought about her all the time, and it was almost true, but nobody heard him. They were skirting the Place de l'Alma and starting up the Avenue Montaigne and Bob was coming to life and Aunt Bonnie diminishing, going down. George sounded like his aunt, inconsequential. When the three separated that night, Flor would be lost. Their conversation and their thoughts were the last of the old Flor. If she was cured, she would be different. He was sure of that.

"You two boys have got to go back for the car," Aunt Bonnie said. "George, you've been a real comfort."

Bob said softly, "I'm glad you came."

They meant it. They would have been glad of anything. They were standing still on a quiet, dark street. This was where Bob and Aunt Bonnie lived. He recognized the double doors leading into the courtyard. He had come there that afternoon, looking for them. "Don't come up," Aunt Bonnie said. "I can get up and into the apartment by myself. I can get out of my clothes and into my bed without any help, and that's all I'm going to do. I'm going to do less and less now. Less and less."

Bob said, "Don't worry, you'll last longer than any of us." He sounded kind.

"Did the walk help you, George?" said Aunt Bonnie, before turning away.

"Help me?"

"I thought you'd had too much to drink, dear. I thought the night air would do you good. That's why I made us all walk." Suddenly she roared with laughter and said, "I must say, I used to adore drunks, I mean witty drunks. I must have, because I married one. Good gracious, when I think of Stanley holding forth, sometimes on the chair and sometimes under it . . ." She kissed George and she went in behind the double doors. George and Harris were alone. George wasn't certain how to behave. He might have said, I'm not drunk, you know, but he was afraid that Bob might answer, Don't worry. George was visiting Paris and Bob was forced to entertain him; it amounted to that. The whole family rose up saying, This man is in hell, be considerate, be decent. There was a lesser but distinct theme: He had no business marrying her. Keep him in his place. George ignored the whisper but he

had heard it all the same. It seemed to him that
the only atonement he could make was to give
Florence back to her husband; to hand her back.
Harris gave him an opportunity. They walked
back to the Avenue Montaigne and stood on the
curb. Harris was watching out for taxis. Suddenly he said, "They might let you see Flor. I
could ask. She might recognize you. It would
be a good thing. You were pretty close, weren't
you?"

This was George's chance and he said the most
considerate thing he could think of, which was:
"To tell the truth, I hardly knew her. I think in
my whole life I only saw my cousin six times."

Handing her back, he renounced all claim to
her. She was outside the family. Harris seemed
unaware of the magnitude of the stroke. He put
up his hand for a cab, which drew up, and they
got in. George was silent. Something had gone
wrong. They rolled back the way they had
walked and on the bridge George had an authen-
tic hallucination. He saw Aunt Bonnie and Flor
and the girl on the Quai Anatole France as one
person. She was a changeable figure, now men-
acing, now dear; a minute later behaving like a
queen in exile, plaintive and haughty, eccentric
by birth, unaware, or not caring, that the others
were laughing behind their hands.